'Have you never been tempted to do something which is wrong?' she demanded, when her accuser continued to glower.

'Yes, I'm tempted to take you out at sunrise and shoot you,' Josh retorted. 'Though it doesn't seem so wrong—it seems more like what you damn well deserve!'

'Why wait until sunrise?' she questioned.

'Because my housekeeper's prepared a de luxe dinner for two and I wouldn't want it to go to waste!'

Books you will enjoy by ELIZABETH OLDFIELD

THE PRICE OF PASSION

Gabrielle's disastrous love-affair with Saul O'Connor had made her look for fulfilment in other areas. Now she had a chain of shops and a beautiful home—she didn't need Saul's love. Or did she?

LOVE GAMBLE

Acting was a risky profession, and risks were the last thing that Roxanne, struggling to bring up her son alone, needed or wanted ever again. But the irrepressible Guy Slaney, who brought such joy into both their lives, was an actor—and loving him would be the greatest risk of all. . .

FLAWED HERO

BY

ELIZABETH OLDFIELD

MILLS & BOON LIMITED
ETON HOUSE 18–24 PARADISE ROAD
RICHMOND SURREY TW9 1SR

All the characters in this book have no existence outside the imagination of the Author, and have no relation whatsoever to anyone bearing the same name or names. They are not even distantly inspired by any individual known or unknown to the Author, and all the incidents are pure invention.

First published in Great Britain 1990
by Mills & Boon Limited

This edition 1990

ISBN 0 263 76817 1

Set in 11 on 12½ pt Linotron Times
01-9009-43804
Typeset in Great Britain by Centracet, Cambridge
Made and printed in Great Britain

CHAPTER ONE

THE schooner swayed beneath her feet. The sun shimmered down. Another perfect day in paradise, Abby thought idly. Across the aquamarine stretch of the harbour a steel band was playing calypsos to welcome passengers from a shiny-white cruise ship, while to her left the little town of St George's, Grenada, basked in the tropical heat. Rising from the curve of the Carenage, houses painted ice-cream colours of vanilla, raspberry and pistachio climbed in higgledy-piggledy steps up the wooded hillside. With its narrow streets and forts, its tranquil anchorage and waving palms, St George's was, so the guidebooks declared, the most picturesque port in the entire West Indies.

'Bob would have been so pleased to know Josh Donner was going to take over the *Calinargo*. He had great respect for him as a sailor,' her aunt said, beside her. Plucking at the feathery silver curls which haloed her head, Hilda Sinclair sighed. 'And he would have been so grateful if he'd known all you've done. Organising the undertakers, notifying our friends, driving me everywhere. I do appreciate it, dear.' Her voice broke. 'I could never have managed without you.'

Abby's fingers tightened around the polished

brass guard-rail. The surroundings might be sublime, but the current situation most certainly was not. A fortnight ago she had flown into the island and, instead of her aunt and uncle, had found a message waiting for her at Point Salines airport: sorry, there was an emergency—please could she make her own way to their bungalow? She could, and she had, and when she had arrived it had been to discover that Robert Sinclair, whom she had never met, had died a couple of hours earlier. A breathing condition which had plagued the elderly American for years had developed into an unforeseen crisis, and there had been nothing anyone could have done. A few days later the funeral had taken place, and subsequently her aunt had asked if she would join her in an evaluation of her finances. What they had found had not been encouraging.

'I'm pleased to be able to help,' Abby said with a smile, for what had to be the hundredth time. She sat herself down beneath the shade of the canopy. 'Tell me about this Mr Donner,' she requested.

Hilda chuckled. 'He's dishy. A young Australian with black hair and the bluest eyes you ever saw. Originally he worked as a lawyer, but he came to the Caribbean on a sailing holiday six years ago and decided to stay. He's single, though I understand he has been married, and——'

'I was referring to his business,' Abby interrupted. Her aunt was incessantly interested in people and loved to gossip, and although she had only lived in Grenada for the one short year of her marriage she seemed to know most of what there was to know about most of the inhabitants. 'Before you phoned him, you said Donner Marine was the major boating company on the island, and I wondered what kind of a set-up it is.'

'Oh. Well, they run a fleet of yachts—ten, I think—which are chartered out. The yachts are white and silver, with air-conditioned cabins, en suite showers, and the latest in radar and such. I'm told they're valued at half a million dollars each.'

'Wow!' Abby exclaimed, knowing she was expected to marvel.

'Each charter is custom-tailored to suit the client,' Hilda continued, 'and such things as fresh flowers, colour television, and a cordon bleu chef to cook the meals are provided. It's luxury all the way. Josh's yard and office are in Cap Mayrellaux, a classy area. He lives in a house nearby which is very classy, too,' she said, unable to resist inserting this snippet of personal information. 'In addition to chartering, the company hire out speedboats, plus they have a number of miscellaneous craft.'

'Mr Donner's gone from tourist to boating supremo in six years?' Abby flicked a strand of pale gold hair from her shoulder. 'He's made it big with remarkable speed.'

Her aunt grinned. 'That's because he's shrewd, and not one for sitting still.'

'He's not one for keeping to time, either,' she

complained, frowning at her watch. 'Your meeting was fixed for eleven, but it's already a quarter to twelve.'

'This is Grenada, dear,' Hilda soothed. 'Here we take life as it comes.' She pointed across the glittering waters of the harbour. 'Josh also owns the *Hummingbird*.'

Abby's grey eyes opened wide. 'He owns *that*!' she protested in horror.

From what she had been told, the dynamic Australian sounded to be the commodore of a sleek and elegant flotilla, yet the vessel being indicated was a cream-painted, square-cornered, tacked-together tub of clumsy proportions. She had noticed it on previous visits to St George's, and had shuddered.

'It's popular with the tourists,' her aunt said benignly. 'Three afternoons a week it sails out to a beach where they can swim and snorkel, and every time it's full.'

'Was the *Hummingbird* operating when Bob ran his cruises?' Abby enquired.

'No. I wasn't here then, but I understand it started up just after he stopped. Josh must have seen the gap which had been left in the market and jumped in. As I said, he's a shrewd fellow.'

Abby inspected her watch again. 'And like I said, he's late!'

'He'll turn up,' the older woman smiled, and wandered off across the deck to chat with Vibert, the grizzle-headed Grenadian who looked after the schooner.

Abby rose to her feet. She tapped out an impatient staccato on the brass rail. She tugged at the collar of the white calico shirt she wore with her khaki miniskirt. She rechecked her wrist-watch. As someone who always arrived on time, who ran herself into the ground to keep deadlines, she did not appreciate being left hanging around—and especially for near enough an hour! Abby drummed on the rail again. Over the past two weeks, she had waited while the doctor had drunk coffee, commiserated, lost and found his records, drunk more coffee. Waited as everyone from the postman to the petrol pump attendant to the woman who ran the local shop had given lengthy eulogies over her uncle. Waited as clerks had completed certificates, waited as the minister had worked his way through every page of the book selecting suitable hymns, waited as the florist had put finishing touches to long-overdue wreaths. She sighed. Grenada was said to be twelve degrees north of the equator and just south of frustration. She agreed.

Tyres screeched, dust swirled, and Abby looked up to see a white Mini Moke coming to an abrupt halt on the quay. Its driver, a tall, dark, shaggy-haired man in a red open-necked shirt and scuffed-up jeans, slid out from behind the wheel and, in long-legged strides, crossed the *Calinargo*'s gangplank and came aboard. With broad shoulders, narrow waist and slim hips, he was, in magazine jargon, all lean-machine.

'Mrs Sinclair,' he said, walking straight to her

aunt, 'I apologise for being late, but an engine went on the blink and fixing it took longer than anticipated.'

'Don't worry about it, Josh.' She smiled.

'I was so sorry when I heard about your husband,' he went on. 'Please accept my condolences. I didn't know Mr Sinclair well, but it was always a pleasure and a privilege to be in his company.'

The grieving widow's eyes filmed over with tears. 'Thank you.'

'You said you wanted to talk to me about selling the *Calinargo*,' he prompted, after a respectful wait during which she sniffed and blew her nose.

'Yes. Yes, I do,' she agreed in a watery voice.

Abby stepped forward. 'We'd like to fix a price,' she said.

Hilda shot her a look of gratitude. At the moment her composure was held together by rubber bands, and once she became distressed she needed time to recover.

'This—this is my niece, Abigail Hammond,' she gulped.

Eyes of an unearthly blue swung her way and Abby found herself being subjected to a thorough and serious appraisal. Very thorough. Very serious. Josh Donner was frowning. It seemed as though one look at her and all manner of internal thoughts, internal decisions, internal doubts had suddenly erupted. Why? she wondered.

'Pleased to meet you, Abigail,' he said finally.

'It's Abby,' she smiled.

'And I'm Josh.'

Although her aunt was a generous-minded soul who tended to specialise in superlatives, Abby had to admit that her description of the tardy Australian had been correct. The eyes which lurked beneath ruler-straight brows were impressive, especially when combined with a broad forehead, square jaw and full, sculpted lips. The man was not only dishy, he had pedigree. Yet it was not his looks which gave Josh Donner an undeniable *potency*—it was the exudation of the kind of authority which comes naturally, completely, and does not need to be advertised.

'My niece flew out from England for a holiday and she's ended up looking after me,' Hilda said, growing misty-eyed again. 'She had hoped to have a chance to rethink her life, but so far all she's done is——'

With a sweep of an arm, Abby exhibited the scrubbed decks, the high masts with their immaculate rigging, the neatly furled sails. 'As you can see, the *Calinargo*'s in excellent condition,' she said, intent on deflecting yet more tears. 'Owing to his health and his travels, Mr Sinclair wasn't able to sail it much over the past year, but he did make sure everything remained in good repair.' She indicated the flat-capped black man who had ambled away. 'Vibert works on the boat daily.'

'And you want an idea of how much she's worth?' Josh enquired, in salty Australian tones.

She shone him a smile. 'We'd like to know how much you're willing to offer.'

'Me?' he said, looking surprised. 'I'm not interested.'

Beside her, she heard her aunt gasp. 'You're—you're not?' Abby faltered.

'No way.'

She stared at him in alarm. Josh Donner was refusing to buy the *Calinargo*? But it had been arranged. He had promised. He *must*. Having married late in life and unexpectedly—a chance meeting with the holidaying Englishwoman had led to instant rapport—Robert Sinclair had announced the intention to show his wife 'a good time'. With this aim—and perhaps due to an unconscious sense of his impending demise—there had been jaunts around the Caribbean, holidays further afield, regular wining and dining at the island's top hotels. Believing her beloved spouse to know best about budgets, about forward planning, about *everything*, Hilda had never thought to query the expenditure, and it had been only after his death she had discovered that the bulk of his capital and most of her savings had gone. As his widow, all she possessed was a head full of memories, a tiny pension from the company Robert had once worked for—and the boat. The boat was vital. The proceeds garnered from its sale would make the difference between severe penny-pinching for the rest of her life and a comfortable old age.

'But when Mrs Sinclair telephoned you said you were,' Abby protested.

He shook his head. 'All I understood was that

you were thinking of selling,' he said, speaking to her aunt, 'and that you wanted my advice.'

'Oh, dear,' Hilda wailed, her face flushed with consternation, 'what am I going to do?'

'You're going to sit here and not worry,' Abby said firmly, 'while I show Josh around. I have no doubt that, when he sees what a beautiful boat this is, he'll soon change his mind.' Marching to the companionway, she beckoned. 'Come along.'

After a moment's hesitation, the Australian followed, clambering behind her up the steps which led to the upper deck.

'I'm sorry about the crossed wires,' he said as he joined her in the sunshine, 'but Mrs Sinclair's conversation was a bit garbled.' He folded brown, muscled arms. 'Where a sale is concerned it's a matter of supply and demand, and you'll realise not everyone has a use for a fifty-year-old, twin-masted schooner.'

'You do.' Abby gestured across the water. 'The *Calinargo* can replace the *Hummingbird*.'

He looked back at her out of unblinking blue eyes. 'Why?'

'Isn't it obvious? Because visitors to the Caribbean would far rather take a sail in a pirate-style galleon like this than chug around in something like—like that!'

'What's wrong with "that"?' Josh enquired.

Although Abby had no wish to offend the man, she did need to persuade him. And, if being blunt was what it took, then blunt she would be.

'It looks like a hamburger takeaway carton!' she declared.

To her relief, he grinned. 'Maybe.'

'I suspect it's not all that special once you get on board, either,' she said, determined to develop the point. Grey eyes narrowed, Abby subjected the floating blemish to a critical scrutiny. 'The deck area looks in need of a coat of paint.'

'It's a while since I was on board,' he said, following her gaze. 'Most of my time's tied up with charters and I'm often away, so——'

'How long is a while?' she demanded.

Josh massaged his jaw. 'Must be near enough nine months,' he said, sounding surprised.

'So you have no idea of the condition?'

His mouth tightened. Her description might have amused him, but this charge of neglect had touched a raw nerve. 'If anything did need painting, Leroy, my captain, would——'

'You could carry twice the number of people on the *Calinargo*,' Abby lobbied, at speed.

'The *Hummingbird* is ticking over nicely, thank you.'

'Ticking over nicely is enough?' she protested.

'Yes. Maybe one day I'll devote more attention to day cruises, but for now I prefer to concentrate on the yachts.'

'Because there's more money in them?' Abby asked, her agitation nudging the query into something suspiciously close to criticism.

'You have it in one,' Josh replied, undaunted.

'They're my bread and butter. And, on the subject of money, I see no sense in laying out a slug on replacing the *Hummingbird* simply for cosmetic reasons.'

End of conversation. End of her sales patter. End of the anticipated straightforward exchange of the *Calinargo* for cash. Abby bowed her head. What happened now? she wondered. If Josh Donner refused to fill his designated role, then an alternative buyer must be found, but when it came to boats and their disposal she and her aunt were novices. How did you get rid of a schooner, one based on a small Caribbean island? Where did you winkle out interested parties? If her father had been alive, she could have co-opted his help, but—she flinched against a jolt of raw remembered anguish—he had died last year. Now her immediate family comprised women, each of whom would be equally ignorant. Abby scooped back the long blonde hair which had fallen over her eyes. Her method was to approach problems from the can-do angle, and she refused to be negative.

'So how does my aunt sell the *Calinargo*?' she enquired.

'She passes the word around the local sailing community, advertises, then sits back and hopes for the best.'

Abby frowned. It sounded very loose, very relaxed, very chancy. 'That's all?'

'What else did you expect?'

She did not know, but she had imagined that,

as an expert, Josh Donner would have been able to come up with something more substantial, something she could not have thought of herself.

'Thank you,' Abby said tartly, 'your advice has been invaluable.'

'Alternatively, you could place the *Calinargo* with a broker or boat agency, if they'll take her on,' he rasped, clearly irritated by her sarcasm. 'However, their fees can be exorbitant.'

'And even if we did, you reckon the chances of a quick sale are slim?'

'Must be.' Josh regarded her in silence. 'Do I take it that Mrs Sinclair is in urgent need of funds?' he enquired.

For a fraction of a second, Abby hesitated. If she had her way the answer would be a frank affirmative, but a mixture of personal pride and embarrassment at her husband's ill-considered spending meant that Hilda was adamant that her financial plight should remain a secret. News travelled fast in a small community, and not only did the thought of pitying glances make her cringe, but she was also determined that nothing—but nothing—should taint Robert Sinclair's memory.

'Good grief, no,' Abby replied, with a merry laugh. 'Whatever gave you that idea? Hilda would simply like to offload the *Calinargo*. It's a matter of——' she shrugged carelessly '—tying up ends.'

Josh frowned. 'OK,' he said, after a moment. 'I'll give her eighty thousand for the damn thing, as it stands.'

Goodbye, anxiety. Hello, joy. Abby wanted to fling her arms around his neck and smother him in kisses. When deciding how much to ask for the *Calinargo*, she and her aunt had considered two things: the first being an offer Robert Sinclair had received some time earlier, and the second, how much Hilda would need in order to decently survive. As both sums had obligingly been within the same area, they had split the difference—though whether the asking price equated with the true value of the schooner had been anyone's guess. However, dishy, blue-eyed, *wonderful* Josh Donner had just offered an amount which was considerably higher!

Although desperate to smile, Abby adopted a carefully crestfallen look. The figure had appeared to have come off the top of his head, so perhaps he could be inveigled into increasing it? Her aunt would always benefit from anything extra.

'Eighty thousand pounds?' she said, as though stricken with ponderous doubts.

'Eighty thousand E. C. dollars,' he corrected.

Abby's sky-high spirits fell to earth with a thud. The wonderful Mr Donner? Forget it. 'Eastern Caribbean dollars?' she echoed, in dismay.

He nodded. 'At today's rate of exchange, that's in the region of——' he did a quick calculation '—seventeen thousand pounds or thirty-one thousand US dollars.'

'But——' she began in protest.

'That—is—my—best—offer,' Josh said, stamping out the words as though engraving them in metal.

Expression sombre, her mind busy, Abby walked to the bow of the boat. Instead of obligingly handing over a cheque, he had thrust her into wheeling and dealing, but she refused to be stampeded. Could Hilda really have been so confused about his agreement to purchase the *Calinargo*? she wondered. It was always possible that wishful thinking had deceived her, and yet. . . Didn't the possibility also exist that the founder of Donner Marine might be the one guilty of deception? She had no wish to malign him, but his switch from lawyer to boat owner and fast-lane zoom up the ladder of success did seem a little slick. In order to have achieved so much so soon, he must be equipped with vast amounts of energy and determination, plus superb opportunistic instincts—if not low cunning.

Abby glanced back over her shoulder. Josh Donner did not look like a man steeped in sin, yet with his intelligent blue stare he did seem entirely capable of turning most situations to his advantage. And hadn't her aunt described him as shrewd?

She nibbled at the inner curve of her lip. So suppose he did want the schooner, and suppose he had decided to obtain it at the lowest possible price? That would explain his initial interest and subsequent claim of crossed wires, maybe his lateness—keep a would-be seller waiting and they can become jittery—and his stout declaration that the *Calinargo* held no appeal—a declaration which he had reneged upon not much later! Abby frowned, her thoughts going back to his look when they had been introduced. At the time she had not understood his wariness of her, but now it became clear. If this meeting had been with her aunt alone, as Josh Donner must have expected, he could have dictated his own terms. His offer would not establish Hilda in a home of her own, nor, if invested, provide much in the way of income, but in her confused state—and because she seemed enamoured of the good-looking Australian—she might well have been persuaded that, no matter how meagre, cash in the hand had its attractions. However, the presence of a niece who was neither confused nor enamoured had caused him some concern. And rightly! Abby thought.

She spun to face him. 'Out of the question,' she declared.

'Who owns this vessel?' Josh enquired.

She stiffened, knowing he already knew the answer. 'Mrs Sinclair,' she said.

'Then shouldn't she make the decision?'

'She will agree with me.'

A quizzical dark brow lifted. 'Yes?'

'Yes!' Abby said fiercely.

'Aren't you being too much the tyrant?' he asked, his smile failing to mask his impatience.

'Aren't you being too much the shark?' she shot back.

He shifted his stance. 'Look, the *Calinargo*

might have been well maintained above the water-line, but what condition is it in below? These islands can rot boats, particularly those which have lain at anchor a long time.'

Struck with visions of the schooner keeling over to sink slowly to the sea-bed, Abby gazed at him in alarm. 'The hull might be leaking?' she ventured.

'Chances are the hull's sturdy enough,' Josh dismissed, 'but in agreeing to buy "as is" I could be saddling myself with a load of repairs, and here it's often difficult and expensive to obtain the right materials.' He nailed her with a stabbing glance. 'In putting up cash like this, I'm doing you a favour.'

'Rubbish! The *Calinargo* is worth at least three times your offer,' she declared.

'If that's what you believe, then advertise the bloody thing!'

'Where do we place the adverts?'

'You want my advice?' Josh demanded blisteringly.

Abby flushed. 'Yes. . .please,' she added, because there was a look in his eyes which warned that he was nearing his limit. If she pushed him any further, he would leave.

'For a start you should try the sailing journals and the newspapers published in the bigger islands—Barbados, Antigua—and in Florida. If you sweet-talk the clerk at the local newspaper office he'll provide the relevant addresses, or he might even circulate an advertisement for you.

Walk upstairs ahead of him in that skirt and there's a distinct possibility he will,' Josh said drily. 'Like me, he's a sucker for long legs, shapely thighs——' He paused, then added incisively, '—et cetera.'

Her flush deepened. In a fit of bravado, Abby had hacked an additional two inches from the mini's original length, but now she regretted it. 'How long do you think it'll take to bring in some enquiries?' she asked, closing her mind to how he had followed her up the companionway and what 'et cetera' might refer to.

'How would I know?' Josh returned. 'All I can tell you is that the last vessel to change hands in this category was on the market for almost a year.'

'A year?' Abby mewed, in alarm.

'You're selling a specialist craft to a specialist market, not flogging a damn fridge-freezer!'

'Yes, but even so——'

'How long are you staying in Grenada?' Josh enquired.

'I came for six weeks, though I could stretch it. I work freelance, so there's no boss anxiously awaiting my return,' Abby explained.

'What do you do?'

'I'm an illustrator.'

'Of what?'

'My last assignment was a series of children's books,' she said distractedly, 'but I've done comic strips, publicity leaflets, sketches for newspapers and magazines. You name it, I'll draw it.'

'A talented lady,' he said pungently.

Abby gave a limp smile. One thing for which she did not possess a talent was putting ancient schooners up for sale, and waiting. While she could stay for two months, or three at a pinch, she could not remain indefinitely, yet neither would she feel happy about leaving her aunt to cope with the *Calinargo's* disposal alone. Their relationship was close—being childless, Hilda's mothering instincts had been diverted to her sister's daughters—and Abby wanted to help, but she also knew that without her support the pliant and somewhat naïve woman would be lost. She cast Josh a slantwise look. In telling her where to advertise he had provided a certain amount of assistance, so was he on the make. . .or not?

'Remember I said the *Calinargo* was worth three times the amount you mentioned?' she queried, deciding that there was nothing to be lost by being honest and open—and possibly something to be gained. 'That was the sum which someone had previously offered my uncle—more or less.'

'When did they offer it?' Josh demanded.

'Eighteen months ago. I know the boat's older——'

'Eighteen months ago Robert Sinclair was running a flourishing day-cruise business,' he cut in. 'That's why the offer was so much higher. The guy didn't want to buy a boat, period. What interested him was a boat, a crew, an established cruise programme, plus the goodwill.'

Abby frowned. 'If the *Calinargo* was still sailing in the afternoons, it'd be worth a lot more money?'

He nodded. 'And it'd be far easier to dispose of. There are always people coming to the Caribbean on the look-out for some kind of business, and a little cruising concern has bags of appeal. A boat and a commercial venture,' Josh summed up. 'You're talking about two different things.'

'So it would pay my aunt to set up in business and then sell?' she mused.

'Yes. Ideally she should be able to provide a year or two's audited accounts, though buyers would be interested as soon as she could show she was running a successful operation. It's that initial launch which folk shy away from.' He shrugged. 'Mrs Sinclair's a sweet old girl, but even if the idea appealed I don't reckon she's capable of getting cruises off the ground.'

'She might not be.' Abby set her hands on her hips. 'However, I am.'

'You?' he demanded, swivelling an intimidating pair of fiercely startled eyes in her direction.

As what had been just a thought began to harden into reality, she dipped her head. 'If the *Calinargo*'s going to be moored here waiting for a buyer anyway, we might as well try to use it to the best possible advantage.'

'But you're an illustrator.'

'You were a lawyer,' Abby countered.

'Maybe, yet I've sailed since I was knee-high. Have you?' Josh thrust.

'I've rowed the odd boat on the odd lake. However, I shan't be taking the helm of the *Calinargo* myself,' she said, ideas beginning to buzz in her head. She peered across the harbour. 'Now, your hamburger carton——'

'The *Hummingbird*,' Josh scythed.

'—services the tourists three days a week, so we'll take them out on the other four. Agreed?'

He paddled a hand through his hair, ruffling the dark curls. 'You can't set up cruises on the spur of the moment,' he protested.

'Why not?'

'Because——' He stopped and began again. 'For a start, the boat'll need to be checked by the authorities to see that she's seaworthy and fit to carry passengers.'

'How long will that take?' Abby asked.

Josh's scowl acknowledged that he had chosen the wrong argument. 'A day—though you might not be able to fix an appointment for a while,' he added belligerently. 'A long while. Have you been to the Caribbean before?' he demanded.

'Never.'

'You just specialise in playing games? OK, it's your choice, but shouldn't you consider that you don't know a damn thing about sailing, or the sea, or——' He changed course. 'The reason the *Hummingbird* goes out just three afternoons is that there isn't the demand for more. We know because we've tried it,' he stated, in an announcement which added a defiant and silent 'so there!'.

Abby frowned. Having recognised a short-term

challenge which could reap long-term rewards, she was in no mood to be deflected, or battered into submitting to his lousy offer. She might have been pitchforked into looking after her aunt's interests, but, like it or not, she would look after them to the best of her ability. She was playing games? If only he knew!

'A romantic boat like the *Calinargo* will tap what, up until now, has been an uninterested market,' she declared.

His jaw hardened. 'You're the one who's being romantic, not to mention fanciful and foolhardy.'

'You think so?'

'I *know* so. You'll never get cruises organised, let alone drum up customers,' Josh proclaimed.

Abby shone him a smile. 'Watch me,' she said.

CHAPTER TWO

ALTHOUGH Hilda had been alarmed when her favourite Australian had bidden her a curt good-bye and made a rapid retreat to dry land, once she had listened to Abby's recital of their conversation—and her scheme—calm returned. As she had bestowed her faith in her husband, so she had no difficulty in agreeing to whatever her niece might suggest—and agreeing with gusto. One of nature's followers, all she required was a leader.

'But the first thing we do is assess expenses,' Abby insisted. In the face of Josh Donner's disdain she had been determined, yet her aunt's enthusiasm made her cautious. 'And if they're too high, we abandon the idea.'

'Bob kept a copy of the *Calinargo*'s cruise accounts on board,' Hilda told her excitedly. 'Let's take a look.'

In the cabin they discovered a full set of records, which included the schooner's running costs, rates for buses to take holidaymakers from and to their hotels, and other outgoings. Admittedly the figures were more than a year out of date, yet they indicated that even when an inflationary increase had been added the initial outlay would still be surprisingly reasonable.

'We go full-steam ahead?' her aunt pressed, when Abby had completed her mental arithmetic.

'Yes, though I'll need to have more funds sent out.'

'I'm financing everything.' Hilda smiled. 'I still have a nest egg, and——'

'No,' Abby objected, shaking her head vigorously. In her role as fully-fledged supporter, the older woman seemed to take it for granted that the cruises would be a smash hit whereas, in reality, they could be a disaster. 'This is my brainchild and I'm paying for it,' Abby said. 'Two years spent hunched over a drawing-board means that, firstly, I've built up a healthy bank balance, and second, I'm desperate for a chance to do something different, something stimulating—and the cruises are it.'

'We'll go halves,' her aunt declared, and no matter how much Abby argued she would not be dissuaded.

'As it's a gamble I suggest we limit ourselves to a six-week trial—that should be enough to assess the demand,' Abby said as they returned to the deck. 'However, we could still advertise the *Calinargo* at the price we fixed. Who knows, we might get lucky.'

'Vibert, we're going to restart the cruises,' Hilda announced, as the black man appeared.

'Cruise again?' His face split into a smile. 'Ain't that jus' great! Spit and polishin' was givin' me fatigue, but to take this baby out on the ocean—now that really is somethin'.'

'Would you be prepared to act as skipper?' Abby asked.

'Delighted, and I got four sons who'll crew. Mr Robert used to say what me and my boys don't know 'bout sailing wasn't worth knowing,' he told her proudly. 'They been limin' round——'

'Doing nothing,' Hilda said, in translation of the local lingo.

'—so they be real pleased to have regular work.'

'It could only be temporary,' Abby stressed, wary of raising false hopes. Briefly she explained, telling Vibert that, should the venture fail, the jobs would also fail—and that if it was successful, she could not guarantee long-term work either. 'In that case, Mrs Sinclair will put the business up for sale and the new owners may prefer to choose their own crew,' she said.

'We take our chance,' the Grenadian replied calmly. Unemployment was high on the island and wages low, so if the chance to earn some money came along you did not hesitate.

'Tell me how Mr Sinclair ran his cruises,' Abby appealed.

Vibert obliged, in wordy detail. 'Mrs Sinclair know 'bout boats operatin' out of some of the other islands, too,' he said, grinning, when he had finished.

'That's right,' Hilda confirmed. 'Wherever we went, Bob always booked a sail. I have the brochures at home. You can read them.'

'Thanks. The more information we have, the

better.' Abby glanced across the harbour. 'It'd be interesting to go on board the *Hummingbird* one afternoon to see how they run things,' she mused.

Her aunt looked worried. 'Wouldn't that annoy Josh? You said he didn't seem too pleased, and——' she fingered the locket she wore around her neck '—isn't it a touch unethical?'

'He must keep up to date on the facilities which other charter firms provide, so I don't see that my monitoring his operation is any different,' Abby defended. In her place, she was sure that Josh Donner would not have pussyfooted around, so why should she? 'Besides,' she continued, 'how will he know I've been? He said he rarely goes on the boat, that he leaves everything to his captain—and as far as the captain's concerned I'm just another holidaymaker.' She patted the older woman's arm. 'Don't fret, I'll keep a low profile.'

'There's no need to book, you can buy a ticket on the quay,' Vibert told her, then added energetically, 'There's a trip the day after tomorrow.'

Abby laughed. 'I'll be on it.'

Arms outstretched, feet neatly together, Abby dived into the crystal-clear depths of the Caribbean. After the burn of the sun, the rush of water against her body was cool, refreshing bliss. Down she went, then, with a kick of her legs, she rose slowly to the surface. Sleeking hanks of wet hair back from her face, she looked around. For well over an hour the *Hummingbird* had sailed along a coastline thick with coconut palms and sea-grape trees, until, rounding a headland, they had entered a small white-sand bay. Here the boat had moored. Now some of Abby's fellow passengers were also swimming, others were diving or jumping into the sea with noses held, while a contingent had donned masks and disappeared to examine the coral. Only a handful, comprising the old, the very young and the lazy, remained on board.

'Enjoy it while you can—it won't last long,' a florid-faced swimmer called to his wife. 'After that late start they'll have to make up lost time, and it'll need to be done here.'

'But I was hoping we could go ashore and explore,' the woman protested.

'Tell that to the captain,' he said sourly.

Abby trod water. Say anything to the captain, and what would be achieved? Sweet nothing. Leroy was smiling, pot-bellied and lazily stubborn—hence 'that late start'. Back at the harbour, they had been on the point of casting off when, somehow, he had dropped his sunglasses overboard. A member of the crew had been instructed to retrieve them and, amid cheers from the passengers, the boy had dived. The water beside the quay had been cloudy—no luck. To the accompaniment of more cheers, he had tried again—and had come up empty-handed. A quarter of an hour later Leroy had still been insisting that he needed his 'shades', and the entertainment had palled. Ten minutes after that, when his mate had been despatched to buy another pair, there had been mutterings of mutiny. The cruise had eventually departed almost forty minutes late.

Abby began a leisurely swim around the boat. Josh Donner's charters might pander to his clients' every last wish, but on his afternoon cruises it was hit-and-miss. Although the tardy start would, presumably, be an isolated incident, there were a number of other grumbles. For instance, the piped music was too noisy and continuous for some; an awning left rolled down on the lower deck restricted the view; the bar service could be erratic. Admittedly, the spectacular scenery and soft sea breezes compensated—and thus the mutiny had soon been forgotten—yet Abby suspected that, if asked later whether they had enjoyed themselves, many of the holidaymakers would reply, 'Yes, but——' That 'but' was significant. Not enough to merit complaints to the management, it could deter others from taking a trip.

Josh's crew were not glaringly inefficient but, left to themselves, they had grown lackadaisical. Only one young man showed much initiative, which meant that he had brought drinks for the older passengers, kept an eye on wandering children, and, when Leroy had been reluctant to provide answers to the many questions, he had taken hold of the microphone and articulately and interestingly pointed out various landmarks. Abby hooked her swimsuit strap back on to her shoulder. Vibert had told her how Robert Sinclair had welcomed people aboard the *Calinargo*, provided a commentary, and generally acted as host—and once again someone was needed to provide this service.

In a swift crawl, Abby reached the ladder and pulled herself aboard. She found her towel, wiped herself down, and padded barefoot to the drinks table where the young man—Eldon, his name badge said—was refilling a bucket with ice.

'I wonder if you can help me.' She smiled, and started to explain the situation and the vacancy.

'I'll do it,' he put in as she paused for breath.

'You?' Although, admittedly, Abby had approached with the idea of offering him the job—as deck-hand, he was disgracefully underused—now she backed away. The young man might fit her requirements to perfection but, tempting though it confessedly was, when it came to the crunch she found that she could not steal him. It would not be proper, or decent, or fair. 'No, no, you don't understand,' she said, hastily covering her tracks. 'I was wondering if you knew of someone else who might be interested.'

Eldon gave a wide grin. 'Me.'

She shook her head. 'You work here,' she insisted.

'Not after today. I've been thinking of quitting for ages, but that messin' round at the harbour fixed it. The minute we dock, I'm telling Leroy this was my last trip. I've been figurin' on driving for a pal who runs a couple of trucks, but I'd prefer to stick with the sea. I'm your man,' he told her. ''Sides, if your cruises don't take off I can do the drivin' later,' he finished pragmatically.

'You're leaving the *Hummingbird* regardless?' Abby checked.

He pressed a hand to his heart. 'Sure am.'

Telephone numbers had been exchanged and a tentative start-up date given, when Leroy bestirred himself and loudspeakered a notice of departure. As Eldon resumed his duties, Abby returned to her seat. It took time for the final passengers to straggle aboard, but then, when everyone expected the anchor to be raised, they waited.

'We're in for another delay,' the florid-faced man groaned, and everyone turned to see a svelte white and silver yacht with turquoise sails cutting purposefully through the water towards them. A couple of youths were talking on deck, but at the wheel stood a tall, tanned man in black shirt and chinos. Abby stared at him in dismay. It was Josh Donner.

Grabbing up her towel and bag, she fled to the tiny cubicle of the ladies' toilet. To pass the time, she stripped off her swimsuit and changed back into her loose cranberry-coloured top and shorts. She had washed her hands, combed her hair, and was applying a touch of lip-gloss when someone rapped on the door.

'Hurry up,' a voice implored.

'I'll be out in a minute,' she yelled, determined to remain in situ until the *Hummingbird* got under way. She grimaced at herself in the mirror. No movement—the engines had yet to be started. How long would this rendezvous last? Not much later, there was a shudder, a rumble, and the boat lurched into motion. With a smile of relief, Abby collected her belongings and opened the door.

'Sorry,' she began, but the waiting woman had already rushed in past her.

On deck, rum punch, the ubiquitous drink of the Caribbean, was once again being distributed, but Abby chose a fresh orange juice. Strolling to the rail, she gazed out at the island where lush green hills rose, tier after tier, up into the clouds. In anticipation of sunset, the sky was filling with shreds of smouldering pinks and peaches and golds. The sea was as calm as a pond. A solitary bird wheeled lazily overhead. She sighed. Paradise again.

'Having fun?' a low voice enquired all of a sudden, and Abby jumped as if she had touched a bare wire.

Josh Donner stood alongside. His blue eyes glittered. His jaw seemed carved from stone. His hand was clenched tight around a glass of mineral water.

'Oh. . .um. . .er. . .' she bleated. She searched feverishly for the yacht, but it had gone. 'You're sailing to St George's with us?' she asked.

'I sure as hell don't intend to swim back!' Josh raked aside the dark hair which the breeze had drifted across his brow. 'So—you decided to check out the opposition?' he demanded.

'I decided to see what the *Hummingbird* offers

in order that the *Calinargo* can offer it, too,' Abby replied, as matter-of-factly as she could. 'It's common business sense.'

'It's common snooping!'

Silence. Tension. Although she tried hard, she could not think of an answer—any answer.

'Have you come to check whether or not the deck needs painting?' she asked, elaborately ignoring his stinging accusation.

'Yes.'

The monosyllabic reply did nothing for her equilibrium, or the tension, or her thought-processes.

'And—and do you think it does?' she enquired lamely.

'Yes.'

Abby beamed a sunburst of a smile. 'I agree.'

'What a surprise.' Josh swigged from his glass. 'Anything else you reckon I should improve on?' he queried sardonically.

'No, no. Everything's fine.'

Abby was telling the truth, in so much as mostly everything was fine—now. As their employer had stepped aboard, so the crew had snapped to attention. The forgotten awning had been neatly rolled, the maudlin muzak had ceased to blare—though after the stop someone could have forgotten to switch it back on again—and the barman was dispensing drinks like an automaton.

'Everything's fine with the *Calinargo*, too,' she gabbled. 'An inspection was made this morning and it is watertight.'

'That was quick,' Josh remarked. 'Trot along to see 'em in your miniskirt, did you?'

'No, I didn't,' she began indignantly, then discovered that he was not listening.

'Sorry to disappoint, but this ploy of yours isn't going to work,' he told her.

Abby frowned. 'What ploy?'

'Don't act the innocent,' he rasped. 'We both know that the only reason you're talking about setting up in business is to try and persuade me to increase my offer.'

'You're wrong! And I'm not talking, I'm *arranging*.'

Josh studied her for a long, frowning moment. 'You actually do intend to resurrect Robert Sinclair's cruises?' he enquired.

'Yes!'

'Gee, thanks,' he drawled. 'I love you, too. You realise that all you'll do is split the market?' he demanded. 'Which means you'll lose out and so will I. Then you'll give up, my cruises'll become profitable again and, after a totally unnecessary débâcle, it's back to square one.'

'I thought you said the *Calinargo* wouldn't attract any customers,' Abby reminded him, her smile sugar-sweet.

A muscle tightened in his jaw. 'I've changed my mind.'

'Then how about changing your mind about my splitting the market?' she demanded. 'Not only must there be people who, for various reasons, aren't free to take a trip on the days the *Hummingbird* sails, but also the number of visitors to Grenada is increasing. I've been to the Tourist Office and checked the figures, and over the past six months there's been a steady surge. I reckon you're underestimating the potential which exists out there.'

'And I reckon you're underestimating what's involved in running cruises,' Josh replied smartly. 'It is not, if you'll excuse the pun, all plain sailing.'

'I'm out of my depth?'

'Totally adrift.'

Her grey eyes sparkled. 'Rocking the boat?'

'Up the creek without a single paddle.' He rested a hip against the rail. 'Isn't it time a little sanity took over?'

Abby sighed. Although turning the *Calinargo* into a business had been an impromptu decision, she had lain awake most of the previous two nights painstakingly considering its feasibility. A whole raft of problems had been envisaged, worked through, surmounted. Now, she was resolved. Where boats were concerned she may be an amateur and an ignoramus, but she had a reasonably intelligent head on her shoulders and setting up cruises couldn't be *that* difficult. Their success, however, was a different proposition. She sighed again. She had also fretted over the rights and wrongs of listening to what Josh Donner had had to say and then using that information against him—sort of.

'I'm sorry if you feel threatened——' she

began, aware of being threatened by her own thoughts.

Josh glared. 'I don't!'

'—but the cruising scene here is not sacrosanct. Indeed, you've been lucky to have had it to yourself for so long. I don't intend the *Hummingbird* to lose trade and I see no reason why it should. However, if it does—well, competition is healthy,' Abby declared, the need to justify her stance welling up inside her. 'It assures the customer of the best possible service.'

'You're championing the consumer now?' he enquired drily.

'I'm explaining that there's room enough for two.'

'You're making all this up as you go along,' he retorted. 'Sweetheart, you may possess an enthusiasm rarely encountered, but you're in cuckoo land. You haven't the first idea about how a schooner——' Josh stopped short. 'I bet you don't even know what *Calinargo* means!'

Her chin lifted. 'Tell me,' Abby requested coolly.

For a moment he hesitated as if tempted to leave her in ignorance, then he started to speak. 'Calinargo or Callinago——' he spelt it out '—is the name the Caribs gave themselves.'

'And the Caribs were?'

'To begin at the beginning, hundreds of years ago Grenada was occupied by the Arawaks. They were peaceful types——' Josh jabbed a thumb in his chest '—like me. Then along came the Amerindians or Caribs. They were a warlike race who raided and ransacked.' He pointed a long brown finger. 'Like you.'

'I'm not raiding and ransacking!' Abby protested.

'No? I repeat,' he said impatiently, 'running cruises is not as simple as it seems. From time to time emergencies occur which may——' He broke off as a member of the crew suddenly appeared beside him. 'Yes?'

''Scuse me,' the man said, 'but there's a couple of dudes fooling around up top and telling everyone they're gonna jump overboard. Bein' a real nuisance, they are. We've tried to calm 'em down but they don't take no notice, and Leroy wondered if you could get tough with 'em.'

'I'll be there in a minute,' Josh assured him. He turned to Abby. 'See what I mean?'

'Yes. Though,' she added, 'that's one emergency which could probably have been avoided.'

His brow furrowed. 'How?' he demanded.

'Those "dudes" are a pair of noisy teenageers who've been downing rum punches ever since they came on board, and the punch you serve is liquid dynamite. I had a glass and it nearly blew my head off. Rum may be cheap in the Caribbean, but when people are sitting in the sunshine gulping down glass after glass they're not too interested in the intoxicant effect—their main requirement is a refreshing drink. One which won't result in them, or others, staggering around, or subsequently being laid low by a giant hangover which makes them curse the day they ever sailed on the *Hummingbird*.'

Josh considered what she had said. 'Sounds as if I'd better tell the barman to tone it down,' he muttered, then cast her a look. 'Thanks.'

'Pleased to be of service,' Abby said lightly.

He dragged his hand through his hair, smoothing down the thick dark curls which grew at the back of his head. 'Why don't you come and have dinner with me one evening, and we can talk some more?' he suggested.

Abby eyed him cautiously. Exactly what did 'talk some more' mean? she wondered. Did Josh intend to embark on yet another attempt to dissuade her from operating the *Calinargo*? If so, he would be wasting his time—and hers. Or might he be planning to quiz her further on his own cruises? If so, he was out of luck there, too. She had pointed out one deficiency—it was up to him to discover the rest. She sneaked him a look from beneath her lashes. His lips had curved and those astonishingly blue eyes were warm. Despite the tale of the Arawaks and Caribs, could he have decided to accept the *Calinargo*'s inclusion in the local cruising scene and live with the consequences?

'Which evening did you have in mind?' she enquired.

'How about me picking you up on Saturday, say around eight?'

Abby smiled. 'That would be fine.'

* * *

Josh's house *was* classy. A long white bungalow with a red fish-scale roof, it sprawled on the top of a hill cleverly taking advantage of whatever breeze was available to stir the air.

'You have a lovely home,' Abby praised, walking with him through the terracotta tiled hall and into a spacious living area.

Here the walls and deep-pile carpet were a white-peach shade, while the suede sofa and chairs were an inky blue. Modern paintings in lime-green, navy and pink added striking patches of colour, she saw twin bronze sculptures of panthers, while in a recess stood a baby grand piano. However, the most stunning feature was the view. Wrought-iron security screens rolled back, the room opened on to a flagstoned terrace, a lawn where spotlights illuminated bushes of violet and mauve bougainvillaea, and, in the distance, the sea. A pale moon hung in the night sky, silvering the ripples on the dark water, the shape of rocks, far islands.

'What can I get you to drink?' Josh asked curtly.

'White wine, please.'

As her host strode towards the kitchen, Abby frowned. After quietening the inebriated youths a few days ago, he had returned to her side. His manner had been easygoing and relaxed. So much so that she had decided that in inviting her to his home he was signalling an end to the hostilities—yet from the moment he had met her this evening he had demonstrated an almost glacial reserve.

'Do you play the piano?' she enquired, on his return.

'You think Australians only wrestle crocodiles and ride surfboards?' he demanded. It could have been a joke, but it was not. 'Yes, I play,' he said, and turned to stare out at the sky.

Abby sipped her wine. Because she had been eager to indicate her willingness to be friendly—and, yes, because Josh Donner was an attractive man—she had devoted much time and trouble to her appearance this evening. She was wearing a chic, strapless grey polka dot on black dress with a tight bodice and a full skirt. Her face had been deftly painted. Her hair was brushed into a shining curtain of pale gold curls which swung halfway down her back. Silver droplets hung around her neck and from her ears. In all modesty, she knew she looked good. Yet he could barely bring himself to glance in her direction!

'Can I ask you something?' she said, deciding to tackle him front-on.

He turned. 'Go ahead.'

'Why are you so "anti" tonight?'

'Can I ask you something?' he thrust back. 'Don't you have any scruples?'

'Sorry?'

'You reckoned you were on the *Hummingbird* to check out what we offered, but,' Josh rasped, his anger spilling over, 'you never told me you were head-hunting!'

'I wasn't. I didn't,' Abby protested.

'Like hell!'

'It's true.'

'Eldon isn't going to work on the *Calinargo*?' he demanded.

'He is, but he'd already decided to leave your employ.'

'You didn't persuade him?'

'No!'

'I can see it all,' Josh said, as though she had never spoken. 'You sashaying up with those big grey eyes and that sexy wiggle and pouring on the charm. The poor bastard wouldn't have stood a chance.'

Abby had always taken a dim view of women who traded on their sex appeal, and now she resented the accusation. 'I don't "sashay" and I don't wiggle,' she said heatedly.

His eyes flickered to her hips. 'Then I must be hallucinating. Please forgive me,' he said, not in the least as though he required forgiveness.

'Eldon was going to quit in any case,' she insisted. 'A friend had offered him a job, but then I mentioned the *Calinargo* and he decided to give it a try instead. Ask him. He'll confirm it.' Ditching the wine glass, Abby found her diary in her bag and leafed rapidly through it. 'There's his phone number,' she said, shoving a page beneath his nose. 'Ring him now!'

'How did you come to "mention" the *Calinargo*?' Josh enquired, sturdily disregarding the scribbled figures.

'I told him about us starting cruises and asked if he knew anyone who might be willing and able to provide a commentary. But I did *not* poach him.'

'The idea never entered your pretty little head?' he said, his voice thick with scorn.

Abby put the diary away. 'Yes, it did,' she admitted ruefully.

'Ha!'

'Though I didn't ask Eldon to join us.'

'Perish the thought!' he jibed.

'And when he suggested it—*he* suggested,' she emphasised, 'I made sure he was already leaving the *Hummingbird*. Have you never been tempted to do something which is wrong?' she demanded, when her accuser continued to glower.

'Yes, I'm tempted to take you out at sunrise and shoot you,' Josh retorted. 'Though it doesn't seem so wrong—it seems more like what you damn well deserve!'

'Why wait until sunrise?' she questioned.

'Because my housekeeper's prepared a de luxe dinner for two and I wouldn't want it to go to waste!'

Abby looked at him. He looked at her. Sneakily, his mouth twitched and so did hers. The twitches spread into grins, and suddenly they were laughing.

'OK, you didn't filch Eldon,' Josh agreed, as he sobered. His eyes crinkled. 'Though you do wiggle.'

'Not much!'

'It's subtle, though in my opinion a subtle wiggle is far sexier than the flaunted kind.' He gestured towards the terrace where a table covered in white damask was set with gleaming glasses and cutlery. 'Shall we eat?'

The food—a mango and prawn appetiser, followed by veal in a spicy sauce, with chocolate mousse for pudding—proved to be delicious. The mood was good, too. Assured of her innocence, Josh became a genial and amusing host, and he also seemed determined to steer clear of talk of cruises—for the time being. As the meal progressed, they discussed her illustrations, his childhood in Australia, places they had been, books they had read, films they had seen. The conversation flowed. There was much laughter. After cheese and biscuits, Josh suggested that they return to the living-room for their coffee.

'A liqueur?' he enquired, bringing in a tray loaded with cups, coffee-jug and cream.

'Do you have a Cointreau?' He nodded. 'I'd like a small one, please.'

He slid her an amused smile. 'You don't intend to be laid low by a giant hangover?'

'Nor do I want to stagger.'

Josh fixed her drink and poured a dash of brandy for himself. 'Mrs Sinclair spoke about you wanting to rethink your life,' he said, joining her on the sofa. 'Does it need rethinking? Your career sounds to be successful, so. . .?'

Abby sighed. 'It's too successful. Don't get me wrong, I'm delighted that people like my work and it's still a thrill to have it published, but the pressure's been such that all I seem to have done for the past two years is draw. I've had no time for holidays, or socialising, or——'

'Men?' Josh asked.

'There was one——' a shadow crossed her face '—but he left. Got fed-up with coming second to a gnome with a bushy grey beard and a bobble on his hat,' Abby said wryly.

'Stiff competition.'

'He didn't much care for the talking mushrooms, whistling ferns and break-dancing oak trees, either.'

Josh laughed. 'You have to give a guy a chance.'

'Yes?'

He stretched out his arm and slowly drew his index finger along her bare shoulder. 'Yes,' he said.

Abby felt the air *crackle*. He was stroking her skin with just the tip of one finger, yet her heart had begun to go b-doyng, b-doyng, her pulse-rate had quickened, she could hardly breathe.

Josh set aside his brandy and cupped her shoulders with two firm hands, then, in what seemed like slow motion, he drew her near, bent his dark head and kissed her. Helplessly, Abby clutched at him, her lips parting to the possession of his mouth and its sensuous, searching need. He gathered her closer, until her breasts were pressed against his chest and she was made tantalisingly aware of how fragile a shield her silky dress and the white poplin of his shirt formed between them. Her nipples tightened. Her skin throbbed.

An ache began to grow. It had been a long time since a man had kissed her—too long—yet surely it had never been as exciting as this? Surely her response had never been so swift, so all-consuming, so fierce?

'Josh,' she murmured, drawing back.

This is too much too soon, she wanted to say. I'm reacting to you too quickly. We must stop. Yet as she gazed at him she recognised a need in the blue of his eyes. It seemed to call to something deep inside her, and that something answered. Abby wrapped her arms around his neck, her fingers pushing into the thick black curls at his nape. Being kissed by him felt so right, she thought, as his mouth opened again on hers. Being held by him created such a yearning that it tugged at all the barriers. Abby stirred restlessly. Without warning, she felt so erotically possessed that it was all she could do not to fling off her clothes and tear at his. She wanted to draw her fingers across his skin, feel the heat of his naked body against hers, inhale his musky male scent. It did not matter that they had only recently met and for most of the time they had been at loggerheads. All that mattered was being held close, feeling the moist pressure of his mouth and the tantalising slide of his hand across the curve of her breast. But as she arched her spine in readiness for a more intimate caress, Josh's fingers abruptly stilled.

'Abby, it's crazy you and me butting heads like

this,' he said. 'Can't we come to some agreement about the *Calinargo*?'

Bewildered, frustrated and locked in the grip of desire, she looked at him. Who cared about the *Calinargo*? she thought dizzily. Why must he talk about the schooner now? How *could* he talk about it?

'What—what kind of agreement?' she asked, struggling to break the spell and force herself back into normality.

'I'll increase my offer.' He frowned. 'Suppose I give your aunt another ten thousand dollars?'

Abby's insides cramped. One minute he had been caressing her, the next he had slid oh, so smoothly into hard-headed business negotiations. She had suspected him of having an ever-ready eye for the main chance, and now there was evidence.

'No, thanks!'

'But you don't even know whether they're E. C. or US,' Josh protested.

'I don't care, and I don't much care for being cold-bloodedly seduced either!' she declared, jumping to her feet.

'Seduced?'

'You invite me here, ply me with food and drink and sparkling conversation, you kiss me, then you slip in an offer for the *Calinargo* and expect dumb acquiescence. Hard luck, buster,' she spat, 'you misjudged.'

But it was she who had misjudged—woefully. When Josh had looked into her eyes and his lips had met hers, his emotions had seemed so real—but it had all been just a piece of theatre. Indeed, she thought miserably, the entire evening had been rigged. The only reason he had invited her into his home was to influence, outwit, manipulate. How could she have been such an unsuspecting fool, and so responsive to his charm? She knew that there was nothing rational about passion, but all it had taken was a couple of kisses and he had reduced her to the proverbial putty in his hands. Abby wanted to howl, or throw bricks, or thump him. She felt furious with herself for having been duped and furious with him for duping her. Her face flamed. She had wantonly and recklessly longed for him to make love to her and, of course, he had known that.

Josh stood up. 'You're making a mistake,' he objected. 'I just——'

'May you rot in hell!' Abby announced, desperate to salvage her pride in some way, any way.

He gave a sardonic bow. 'Thank you. I thought that, as I'm going off on a charter tomorrow for a month, it would be a good idea to have things settled,' he continued.

'Things *are* settled,' she declared, her voice precision-tooled. 'And if the *Calinargo* does take some of your customers, so what? You won't be forced into abject poverty.'

'That's not the issue. Our——'

'Why did you quit the legal profession?' she asked abruptly.

'What's that got to do with anything?' he demanded.

'I assume it was because when you arrived in Grenada you saw an irresistible chance to get *much* richer *much* quicker with boats?'

He scowled. 'No. I admit I was in the right place at the right time, but——'

'I can imagine,' Abby said succinctly.

'As I was saying,' Josh rapped, becoming impatient of her hostility, 'our busiest season's looming, which means Donner Marine have a hell of a lot of plates to keep spinning in the air and, frankly, I don't have the time to waste on pointless hassle.'

'Too bad!' Blonde head held high, Abby stalked to the door. 'I don't have any more time to waste on this evening either, so I would be obliged if you'd take me home.'

CHAPTER THREE

THE qualms Abby had harboured about infringing on Josh Donner's trade were now banished. Having shown herself to be vulnerable and having been exploited, her determination to make the *Calinargo*'s outings a success was intensified. Not only would she do her damnedest on Hilda's behalf, but she would also show him that she was a force to be reckoned with. From here on they were not merely competitors—it was *war*, and Abby intended to employ all the ammunition she could.

'How about us starting the cruises mid-morning, finishing mid-afternoon, and serving a buffet lunch?' she suggested to her aunt, the next day. 'We could prepare, say, chicken casserole, heat it up in the galley and serve it with a range of cold meats, savoury rices and salads. If we offer a decent spread we can charge more and increase the profits,' she went on, the lustre in her eyes signalling a Messianic verve. 'Most people are happy to spend on holiday so long as they're getting value for money, and we'll make sure they do. If we rope in a couple of girls, the four of us should easily handle it.'

'Sounds a splendid idea,' Hilda agreed.

Abby opened a folder and took out a sketch

she had made. 'How about this as the basis for our advertisement?' she asked.

A tubby, bewhiskered pirate smiled from the deck of the *Calinargo*, another waved in the rigging, a third beamed hello at the prow.

Her aunt chuckled. 'It's fun.'

'We could have T-shirts printed with the picture and the name of the boat in bold letters,' Abby continued. 'Then the crew could wear them, passengers could buy them, and the cruises would be advertised for free. What do you think?'

Stricken by a rare sensation of disagreement, the older woman hesitated. 'As it's just a trial, I suspect, dear, you're being a touch too ambitious,' she said gently.

Abby pulled a face. 'You're right,' she agreed.

'In any case, I can't think of anywhere on the island which would produce that kind of thing. We'll need paper plates and plastic cutlery for the lunches, but I doubt whether we can rely on finding a local source, either. Not a continuous one. Grenada is only a dot on the map. I've got it,' her aunt said, suddenly brightening. 'One of my bridge partners is going over to Barbados tomorrow; I'll ask her to bring back a supply.'

In the days which followed, other snags revealed themselves—and, one way or another, were overcome. The schooner was decked with bunting. Hilda switched many of her kitchen utensils to the galley. One of Vibert's sons agreed to do duty as barman. Abby completed the advertisement, oversaw its printing, then sped from hotel to hotel, from one apartment block to another, feverishly distributing notice-board bills and leaflets.

'We start next Tuesday,' she recited until her vocal cords were strained and, as back-up, stapled the advertisement to a number of roadside trees and bus shelters.

The big day arrived. Having dashed around from dawn until dusk for two weeks, Abby awoke feeling tired and twitchy, and as the morning progressed it was sheer adrenalin which kept her functioning. Fifty passengers had been expected and when only forty-four climbed off the buses, her world collapsed. The schooner would carry a hundred, and while she had been content with half a load, to have mobilised less seemed pathetic. Despair made a rusty pain in her chest. Josh had been right. The cruises *were* nothing but a pointless hassle—for him, for her, for everyone. Why had she ever had such an insane idea? Then a group of vacationing Germans appeared. 'Can we join you?' they asked, and—snap!—the rusty pain vanished, the tiredness fled, her day was one of unalloyed pleasure.

The next time out, they mustered sixty passengers. Sixty-five assembled for the cruise after that. And seventy on the fourth excursion. If only Josh Donner were around to see us now! Abby thought as the schooner sailed serenely back through the narrow entrance into the harbour. On the upper deck, Eldon was relating the island's history to a group of avidly listening holidaymakers. On the lower, people were drinking portion-controlled rum punches, or congratulating the girls and her aunt on the tasty lunch, or admiring the view. The *Calinargo* was in business!

'Any idea how the *Hummingbird*'s doing?' she asked Vibert at the end of the following week.

On the days when they were not sailing, she and Hilda divided their time between recovering from the last cruise and preparing for the next, so there had been little chance to keep track of the opposition. Though, in all honesty, Abby had not wanted to keep track. Indeed, the more successful the *Calinargo* became, the less inclined she was to know how Josh's business was faring. Yet to start having qualms again was ridiculous. The important thing was to secure her aunt's future, and both of them were suitably cock-a-hoop because thus far the prospects looked rosy.

The Grenadian gazed across the harbour. 'Not well. I counted and there were only twenty folks on board when it went out yesterday. Mr Donner ain't goin' to like it,' he prophesied cheerfully.

'Then Mr Donner will have to lump it,' Abby replied, telling herself that there was no reason to feel guilty.

'How many passengers we expectin' this morning?' Vibert enquired.

'Seventy again,' she grinned. 'So I'd better get back down to the galley and help with the food.'

Although who did what on the catering side had rapidly been established, providing multiple lunches required dedicated preparation and as the schooner sailed along the coast a variety of tasks were tackled. The rice was cooked, tomatoes and cucumbers diced, paper napkins were folded around endless knives and forks. Once they had moored and the bulk of passengers had departed to pursue the various water pleasures, the girls set up the buffet table in the prow, while Abby and her aunt kept pace providing plates of meat, huge assortments of salad, bowls of mayonnaise and vinaigrette.

'Ready for serving duty?' Hilda asked, as the swimming and the snorkelling came to an end and the decks began to fill again.

Abby neatened the line of her chalk-blue shirt, lifted heavy skeins of golden hair from her shoulders, and saluted.

'Yes, ma'am.'

Joining the two girls, she readied herself to serve the chicken while her aunt took her place lower down the table behind a tureen of rice. A few moments later, Eldon announced that lunch was ready and a queue rapidly formed. With a smile for everyone, Abby began to dispense helping after helping after helping. A procession of plates was filled, time passed, the queue dwindled.

'No choice?' one of the last customers enquired as he arrived at the table.

Head down, back bent, Abby was lifting a full dish to replace yet another empty one. 'Sorry, not of hot food,' she replied, in answer to a question she had been asked before. Digging deep, she brought out a spoonful of chicken chunks floating in a rich herb sauce. 'But I can recommend the casserole, it's. . .' Her voice trailed off. 'Your—the charter's finished?' she asked unevenly.

'My clients departed happily for home last night.' Josh scoured the aft deck where groups of people were sitting eating. 'Yours seem pretty contented, too.'

Abby's spine stiffened. 'You've come to increase your offer for the *Calinargo*?' she demanded.

'No.' His eyes drilled into hers like blue steel. 'Neither am I about to seduce you.'

It took an effort, but she forced herself to look steadily back. 'Then why are you here?' she asked.

'To check out the opposition. It's common business sense.'

For a second time, Abby was bereft of an answer.

Josh's gaze swept over the buffet table. 'I trust one extra isn't going to wreck the fine-tuning of your catering arrangements?' he drawled.

'It won't. We have plenty.'

'That's a relief. Please, go ahead,' he said, turning to smile at a stocky, Bermuda-shorted woman who had ambled up behind him.

The woman smiled back and thanked him—excessively, Abby thought. It was not as though Josh had presented her with a diamond tiara, merely a place in front of him.

'Chicken, madam?' she offered, going through

her paces. 'Would you like some?' she asked, when his admirer's plate was laden and she had shuffled along in search of salad and rice.

Josh hooked his thumbs in the slit pockets of his jeans. 'Would you like some chicken, *sir*,' he said.

Abby glowered. With his hips thrust forward and the denim stretched tight across his thighs, he looked all masculine, all physical, aggressively sexual.

'You are here to give the customer the best possible service,' he chanted, sing-song fashion. The corner of his mouth twitched. 'Read me?'

'Like a comic book!' She grabbed up a paper plate. 'Would you like some chicken, *sir*?' she growled.

'Please.' As if by a switch, his amusement snapped off. 'How come you've changed the rules?' Josh demanded, standing erect.

'What rules?'

'When you talked about servicing the tourists on alternate days, I innocently assumed it would be on an equal basis, that is, afternoon cruises. Instead of which——'

'Josh!' her aunt exclaimed, a dearth of customers allowing her to suddenly catch sight of him. She shone an uncertain smile down the table. 'You've come to see how we're getting along?'

His helping of chicken secured, he moved towards her. 'I already know—a report of the *Hummingbird*'s receipts gave me *that* information,' he said drily. 'But I wanted to discover the reason for your success. Laying on lunch was a smart piece of thinking.'

'It was Abby's idea,' Hilda told him, dithering between a pride in her niece's initiative and dismay at the thought of his dwindling passengers.

'I assumed it would be,' Josh replied. 'A one-girl think-tank, is she?'

'Oh, yes. She suggested we sell T-shirts with a picture of the *Calinargo* on the front. That way we'd——'

'If you don't hurry, the chicken will go cold,' Abby interrupted, shooting you're-being-indiscreet messages down the table. The T-shirt scheme might have been abandoned, but that was no reason to give him the benefit of her inspirations!

Hilda looked flustered. 'More rice, Josh?' she asked hurriedly.

'No, thanks.' He smiled, and walked away.

A hungry few returned for second helpings, but in due course lunch ended, the used plates and cutlery were collected in plastic sacks, the table was dismantled. Vibert resumed his position behind the wheel and the schooner set sail. Down in the galley, Abby did her share of the washing, the drying, the tidying-up. As she had gone on to Josh's boat and learned what *not* to do, so he had come aboard the *Calinargo* and learned what *to* do, she thought grimly. Blast it! Blast him! Maybe it meant that they were quits, but knowing he was on board made her edgy.

'How is everything?' she asked Eldon, when he came in for something to eat.

'Smooth, real smooth, apart from a middle-aged guy who's complainin' of not feelin' too good.'

'What's the matter with him?'

'Dunno, but he's turned a nasty greeny-white colour.'

'I'd better see if there's anything we can do,' Abby decided.

'I'll come, too,' Hilda said.

Up on deck the man, a portly, grey-haired Londoner, was slumped on a bench with his wife beside him. Sober-faced and pallid, a greasy film of sweat glistened on his brow.

'I feel lousy,' he told Abby, in response to her query.

'Perhaps it's something you've eaten,' her aunt suggested.

'Doubt it.'

'Or you could have had too much sun.'

His wife, a sharp-faced woman in a plaited-straw hat, shook her head. 'Raymond's having one of his bad turns, that's all. He gets them from time to time.'

'Not turns like this,' he objected, rounding on her. 'I've never had a tightness in my chest before.'

A tightness in his chest? Immediately Abby's thoughts flew back to another time when she had heard that phrase. 'You—you think there might be something seriously wrong?' she faltered.

'It's possible,' he said.

'Raymond, you've just been too energetic in your swimming,' his wife grumbled.

Abby gave a gaudy smile. 'Suppose I ask Eldon to enquire whether we have a doctor on board? Just to be on the safe side.'

The sufferer grimaced. 'Please do.'

The message boomed out, but no doctor appeared. All the announcement brought were one or two inquisitive types who goggled, offered a judgement, and went away.

'Is your chest still painful?' she fretted.

The man pressed a hand to his side. 'I feel like death,' he replied.

Death? Her heart lurched. The world tipped. Everything went out of synch. As the schooner rounded a headland and the specks of buildings which made up St George's came into view, Abby trembled. The town looked so distant, so remote, so unattainable. Even with them sailing at full speed it would take an hour and a half to reach it, but *anything* could happen in that time, she thought—remembering, remembering.

'Need some help?' an Australian voice asked, and she swivelled to see Josh arriving from the upper deck.

Tempted to utter a snappy 'no, thanks' and send him on his way, she hesitated. 'This gentleman is feeling ill and——' a jerk of her head drew Josh with her a discreet distance away '—I think he could be heading for a coronary.'

He frowned at the man, frowned at her. 'Why do you say that?'

'He's complained about a tightness in his chest.'

'That's all?' She nodded. 'You're over-reacting,' Josh said. 'Sure, the guy looks a bit off-colour, but——'

'He could *die*,' Abby hissed.

'Cut it out,' he protested.

'He could.' She felt the inward beat of distress. 'You warned me about emergencies, but I never visualised anything as—as dramatic as this!'

Josh gave an irritated sigh. 'It's you who's creating any drama. If one of your passengers happens to feel under the weather it's not your fault, so if what's worrying you is him suing, forget it.'

'What I'm worried about is him having a heart attack!' she said through gritted teeth. 'We're stuck out on the ocean, it'll take forever to reach the harbour, never mind medical assistance, and coronaries can strike in minutes. Oh, Josh,' she wailed, giving way to her fears, 'what do we do?'

He flung her an exasperated look. 'You don't panic.'

'I'm not! I'm just——'

'In a heightened state of mental awareness?' he defined drily.

The man suddenly winced, pressed a white-knuckled fist to his chest and gave a loud groan.

'There you are!' Abby cried. Her eyes flew to the shore. 'Maybe we should land and try to get help.'

'Where?' Josh enquired. 'From whom?'

Frantically she surveyed the coastline, but all she could see was a hillside thick with palm trees. There were no houses, no people, no obligingly sited telephone boxes.

'What would your crew do if someone was dying on the *Hummingbird*?' she implored, taut with frustration.

'Abby, the likelihood of that guy cashing in his chips right now is minimal!'

'You're a doctor of medicine as well as law?' she demanded.

'What I am,' Josh said harshly, 'is certain you're——'

'That man is overweight, in his fifties and there's nicotine on his fingers, so he smokes. He's the perfect candidate for a heart attack—yes?'

'I guess,' he said reluctantly, 'but——'

'And heart disease is a major killer.'

'Even so——'

'He needs medical attention!' Abby insisted, and heard her voice shrill. She brought it down to a more reasonable level. 'He *does*.'

Josh gave a long drawn-out sigh. 'How'd it be if I make radio contact with my yard and have someone come out here in a fast boat?' he suggested. 'We could transfer the guy, deliver him to an ambulance which would be waiting at a pre-arranged landing point, and have a doctor examine him—if you're desperate.'

Abby *was* desperate. 'Oh, yes, please,' she said,

almost blabbering with gratitude. As he disappeared to speak to Vibert, she returned to the couple and explained what would be happening.

'That's very kind.' The man's wife smiled. 'Though I don't really think Raymond needs——'

'Better to be safe than sorry,' the sufferer said, speaking over her.

Although contact was quickly made and Josh returned with the assurance that someone had already set off, Abby spent the next half-hour in a state of high anxiety. Josh might point out that the man had had no further pain attacks and that his colour was returning, but this was, she insisted, no guarantee that his condition would not suddenly deteriorate. Please make the boat hurry, she implored silently, and when, at last, it appeared on the horizon she felt weak with relief.

'I'd like to accompany them,' she told Josh as the speedboat approached. 'I need to know everything's all right.'

'Whatever you wish,' he said in weary resignation, then added, 'I'll come, too.'

Abby's chin lifted. 'So you're worried?' she challenged.

'Only about you and your blue funk,' he replied.

The *Calinargo*'s engines fell silent, the speedboat came alongside, and, while the other holidaymakers watched over the rail, the man was helped aboard.

'You don't know how long you'll be at the

hospital, so I'll take a taxi home,' Hilda said, as Abby made to follow. 'Can you pick up Bob's car from the quay?'

'Will do,' she assured her.

The boat shot off, moving at speed but steadily, and not much later they reached a jetty where an ambulance was waiting. A quarter of an hour after that, they were at the hospital.

'I can't tell you the cause of his distress until we've done a few tests,' the doctor said, as the Londoner was taken into a consulting-room. 'Are all you folks intending to hang on?'

'I am, but there's no need for you to stay,' the man's wife told Abby and Josh. She gave an embarrassed smile. 'Raymond's feeling much better now, and he is a bit of a hypochondriac and, to be honest, he does make a fuss over nothing.'

'None of which means that this is nothing,' Abby said, her face grave.

'I suppose not,' the woman admitted grudgingly.

'I'll wait with you,' she declared.

'No way,' Josh objected and, taking hold of her arm, he marched her rapidly to the door. 'We both have cars which need to be collected,' he flung over his shoulder, 'so we'll be back later.'

'There's no need to manhandle me!' Abby protested, as he bundled her through the entrance hall and out down the steps. Furiously, she twisted free. 'Neither do I need you to make my decisions. Maybe you want to pick up your car right now, but for me it isn't important. What is important——'

'Is keeping that guy's wife from becoming a nervous wreck like you!' he blasted. 'If you stay with her, chances are you'll infect her with your anxiety and have her believing her husband's on the brink of a coronary, too.'

'But he could be,' she insisted.

'And you could be the owner of an overactive imagination!' In long strides, Josh set off for the gate. 'Tell me, do you always go to pieces the instant anyone turns pale?' he demanded, his voice as sharp as an ice-pick. 'Because if so I suggest you pack in the damn cruises as from today.'

'You don't understand,' Abby muttered, needing to hurry in order to keep up with him.

'No, I don't! I might not be thrilled with your spectacularly successful launch, but it did appear to show you had resourcefulness and spirit, that you could cope. Cope?' His lip curled. 'Get you on the high seas, lady, and you're nothing but a menace. Inept. Incapable. At the first hiccup you dissolve into hysterics. You——'

'Wanna taxi, Mr Donner?' someone shouted, and Abby looked up to see a young Rastafarian, his dreadlocks covered by a huge yellow bonnet, grinning from a car which had slowed outside on the road.

'Please,' Josh replied, and, forced to curtail his denouncement, he satisfied himself by flinging her a scurrilous look. 'We'd like to go to the Carenage, Lloyd,' he said as he ushered Abby inside.

With a nod and a squeal of tyres, they sped away.

'How you makin' out?' the young man asked, beaming at Josh through the mirror.

'Fine. And you?'

One question, two words, but they were all the prompting Lloyd needed to embark on a recitation of the more recent events in his life. With frequent backward glances and a noticeable lack of road sense, he spent the journey skidding around corners, bouncing through pot-holes, narrowly avoiding other traffic, and talking, talking, talking. Even when they arrived at the harbour his tale continued, until a new customer appeared and demanded a ride.

'Thank you for your assistance,' Abby said stiffly as she and Josh walked towards the parked cars. 'If you let me know how much I owe you for the use of the speedboat and driver, I'll——'

'There's no charge,' he told her.

'But——'

'Everyone pitches in at sea. Besides, maybe there'll be an occasion when you can help me,' he said, in tones which equated the likelihood with pigs taking wing.

Abby unlocked Robert Sinclair's small Ford. 'Goodbye, then,' she said.

'No.' Josh shook his head. 'I'm going back to the hospital with you.'

She frowned. After relying on him so heavily, she was eager to demonstrate her independence—

and the ability to cope. 'That's not necessary,' she protested.

'You don't want me around to help dig the guy's grave?' he demanded ghoulishly.

She flinched. 'I don't want you to waste any more of your time,' she replied. 'When's your next charter?'

'I leave tomorrow for a week, then I'm back for a couple of days, then I'm away for another week.'

'So you obviously have plenty to do.'

'If you think I'm going to leave you alone with that guy's wife—forget it!' Josh installed himself behind the wheel of the Moke. 'Follow me,' he ordered laconically. 'I'd hate you to get lost and go into a frenzy.'

Back at the hospital, Raymond's wife had nothing to report. 'I thought he was exaggerating the pain,' she said, removing her straw hat and frowning at it, 'but he's been with the doctor for so long that now I'm beginning to wonder.'

Josh gave a disarming grin. 'Don't,' he said. 'You're in Grenada, where delays are par for the course.'

'Everything happens at a much slower pace,' Abby put in, and was rewarded by his imperceptible nod of approval. 'Have you done much sightseeing while you've been here?' she enquired conversationally.

The woman smiled. 'We've been everywhere. One day we hired a car and drove all around the island. Another time we went inland to see some waterfalls and a lake. We've called in at a nutmeg factory, and had lunch at an old plantation house. We've toured the market, and Fort George, and——' Now into her stride, she proved to be as garrulous as Lloyd. 'We've been here a month, but I'm still sorry to be going home tomorrow,' she said. The end of her diatribe had appeared imminent, but she took a breath. 'Talking about delays,' she carried on, 'the day after we arrived—the eighth, it'd be—Raymond and I went on the *Hummingbird*—this was before we'd heard about your boat,' she informed Abby in an apologetic aside. 'And just as we were setting off the captain dropped his sunglasses in the water. We were made to wait ages while the silly fellow had someone dive, and then——'

'Mild angina,' the doctor announced, striding into the waiting-room in his white coat. Raymond's wife blinked. Her sightseeing reminiscences had been so engrossing, she had almost forgotten why she was here. 'Angina pectoris, that's why your husband was in pain,' he explained. 'For the most part it arises in connection with disease of the coronary arteries.'

'Oh, dear,' she said, in sudden alarm.

The doctor smiled. 'Don't worry; I stress—the angina's mild.'

'Then there wasn't any real emergency?' she asked.

'No.'

Josh shot Abby a glance. 'And no danger of a heart attack?' he queried.

'None. The patient's fine now, all he needed was some rest and a tablet. I've given him a supply of tablets and told him to consult his own physician as soon as he gets home,' the doctor continued, addressing the man's wife. 'He must learn to slow down and not over-exert himself, and—there you are,' he said, as Raymond walked in. 'He'd be wise to shed some weight. A taxi's been organised to take you back to your hotel, so, now that everything's settled——' he held out a hand '—goodbye.'

'Thank you,' Raymond said, and after a brief exchange the doctor departed. 'Thank you, and thank you,' he repeated, nodding at Abby and Josh. He gave a shamefaced grin. 'Sorry to have caused so much trouble, but——' He shrugged. 'Can't keep the taxi waiting,' he told his wife, and backed hastily out of the door.

'Go ahead, say it,' Abby demanded, the moment they were alone.

'What, I told you so?' Josh shook his head. 'The only thing I want to say is—how did you know the guy's heart was at fault?'

She drew in an unsteady breath. 'Because less than a year ago I was with my father when he complained of chest pains.'

'And?' he prompted, as the remembrance held her silent.

'And—and fifteen minutes later he was dead.'

Josh winced. 'Oh, God! I'm sorry. So that's why——'

'I went "to pieces"?' Abby quoted. 'Yes,' she

said, and marched from the room and out to the car park.

'Would it help if you told me about your father?' Josh suggested, as they reached the cars.

She frowned at him, then contemplated the keys she held in her hand. When her father had died, her mother had been so distressed and in need of so much support that her own grief had been stifled. For months she had comforted and sustained, and as her mother had slowly begun to recover Abby had also believed that she had put the trauma behind her. It was not so. Albeit Robert Sinclair was a stranger, his death had dislodged an emotional log-jam and made her unhappily aware of unresolved hurt and loss. She looked at Josh again. She was not sure why she should want to talk to *him*, but all of a sudden the chance to explain about her father seemed not so much appealing as a necessity.

'Yes.' Abby gave a small smile. 'Please.'

'Let's sit in the Moke.'

'My mother was at an evening class, and my sister had gone camping, and I'd called round, and—and Dad and I were in the house alone,' she began hesitantly, when she had climbed in beside him.

'You have just the one sister?' he interrupted.

'Yes. She's training to be a teacher and she lives at home. Dad was telling me about some restaurant he'd been to which had menus in indecipherable French and toffee-nosed waiters,' Abby continued, 'when suddenly he stood up, took a few steps and then——' she swallowed '—he crashed to the ground. He lay there writhing and gasping in tortured breaths, and—and I was terrified to leave him, but I had to ring for an ambulance. I ran into the hall and phoned, and when I came back his face was contorted and he was swearing. Dad rarely used bad language, and to hear him then seemed so shocking. It made me realise the agony he was in.'

'You must have been pretty distraught, too,' Josh murmured in sympathy, and she nodded and blinked away tears.

'Somehow I managed to get him into an armchair,' Abby went on, 'and for a short time it seemed as though he could be recovering. But then he gripped his chest and swore, and——' she stared straight ahead '—and I tried thumping at his heart, I tried mouth-to-mouth resuscitation, but he was dead before the ambulance arrived.' She took a shuddering breath. 'Like my father, Raymond is in his late fifties, heavily built and he has the same wavy iron-grey hair.'

'And when you saw him you thought history was about to repeat itself?'

Abby nodded bleakly. 'All the sensations of terror and helplessness and doom came flooding back. At home I'd been able to ring for an ambulance—not that it had altered anything—but out on the *Calinargo* I didn't have a clue what to do.' She looked at him. 'You were right, I did panic.'

Josh's fingers gently enfolded her hand. 'It was understandable.'

'But I won't panic again,' she declared.

'What would you do if there was an emergency?' he enquired.

She thought for a moment. 'I'd ask Vibert to contact the coastguard and request their help. Yes?'

Josh grinned. 'Yes.'

'I'm so glad everything turned out all right,' Abby said shakily. She looked down at the strong brown hand which held her own. 'And I'm so glad you were there. I appreciate what you did for me today, how you——'

'Hey,' he murmured as she broke off, the tears once again glistening in her grey eyes.

'I'm grateful,' she mumbled, and lurched forward, grabbed him to her, then, a split second later, jerked back.

What was she doing? Abby wondered, in pink-faced confusion. Josh might have helped her and lent a sympathetic ear, but that was no reason for dragging him into a clinch. She frowned. She might not trust him, but neither, it seemed, could she trust her own responses!

'Was that a cuddle or a kidney punch?' he asked.

'It was a thank-you,' Abby replied, stiff-backed and prim.

'Sure you're not trying to seduce me?' he asked, the tilt of a smile showing in the corner of his mouth. 'You don't intend to rip the buttons off my shirt and cast my string vest to the winds?'

'No.' Swinging her feet to the ground, she gave

an embarrassed smile. 'See you around some time. Goodbye.'

With a noisy grind of gears, Abby drove away. She needed to put space between them—and quickly. Why did Josh Donner have such a disturbing effect on her? she wondered. Why had she felt compelled to touch him? And it *had* been compulsion. Foot pressed down, she swept around the blue glass oval of the lagoon and up over the hill. A long, slow bend, a left turn on to winding, hedged lanes, and eventually she drew to a halt outside her aunt's apricot-coloured bungalow.

'I'm back,' she called, walking inside, 'and you'll be pleased to know that the man's fine. He——'

A note on the desk brought her up short. Hilda had 'popped out' to see a friend and would be back in five minutes. Abby smiled. Her aunt's five minutes invariably lasted a full hour.

Although the day had begun to fade, the temperature remained in the eighties, so she poured herself a glass of pineapple juice from the fridge and added ice-cubes. She wandered back to the desk. She had come to the Caribbean with the intention of not putting pencil to paper, but the advertisement sketch had prompted some ideas and in spare moments she had found herself jotting. She had drawn cameos of West Indian life—a woman carrying a tray of bananas on her head, a skinny youth stomping along in thick-soled flip-flops, a schoolgirl with sticky-out pigtails. Switching on the ceiling fan, she sat down and began to draw the taxi driver with his knitted bonnet.

'I'm in here,' she called a few minutes later when footsteps sounded in the hall. Abby pushed her hands beneath the mane of blonde curls and raised them from her neck, cooling her skin. Body stretched, she waited for her aunt to appear—and was astonished when Josh walked in instead. 'Shouldn't you knock?' she demanded, annoyed to feel an instant *frisson*.

'I did,' he said, his eyes fastening on the uplifted tilt of her breasts, 'but there was no reply.'

'Oh.' Abby released her hair and sat up straight. 'What do you want?' she demanded.

'The eighth,' Josh said, walking over to where she sat. 'I'd almost reached the yard when it registered that that was the day you went on the *Hummingbird*.'

'So?'

'How long did Leroy delay the start?'

'Why don't you ask him?' Abby hedged.

'Two reasons,' he ground out. 'One, I'm not entirely convinced the bastard would tell me the truth, and, secondly, I don't have time to chase him up.'

'The cruise left forty minutes late.'

'Thank you.'

'Anything else?' she enquired, wishing he would not stand so close.

'Yes. I noticed your advert offering the *Calinargo* for sale. Had any takers?'

'Not yet,' Abby said crisply.

Josh looked down at her drawing. 'That's good,' he grinned. 'Theo needs someone like you.'

'Who's Theo?'

'One of the guys who skippers for me. He's written a handbook on sailing in the Caribbean, but the publishers require some illustrations,' he explained. 'Theo's no artist himself so he's been persuading all kinds of folk to submit drawings, but so far none of them suits.'

'Poor Theo. Is that it?' Abby demanded, impatient for him to leave.

'One more thing.'

'Which is?'

Josh walked to the doorway where, hands in his pockets, he leaned a casual shoulder. 'I figure it's time you knew what it is that freaks you out about me.'

'Freaks me out?' she repeated, wary of how his mouth had curved.

'Yes. It's my sexuality,' he told her, his blue eyes bright with laughter. 'It plays havoc with your peace of mind.'

Abby glared. 'You are the most——'

'Whoops,' he murmured, 'did I say something wrong?'

An india rubber was grabbed up and flung. 'Go,' she yelled. She despatched a handful of pencils which scattered in all directions. 'Leave!' She hurled her crayon box, and was furious when Josh moved sideways and she missed him—again. 'Get out!'

CHAPTER FOUR

ALTHOUGH a lifelong landlubber, Abby now offered up a devout thank-you for boats. The next day, one of his luxury yachts accommodatingly removed Josh Donner from the island, while her involvement with the schooner left little time to dwell on him and his statement—which would not have been so infuriating had it not, unfortunately, been true.

However, as the days passed each excursion in the *Calinargo* inevitably honed the general expertise and, where the lunches had started as a mammoth undertaking, another week on found them being swiftly and routinely prepared. No longer rushed, Abby found herself thinking in plenty.

On the personal side, it made sense to avoid further contact with Josh and, courtesy of his well-nigh continuous charters, that would be easy to do. But how did she tackle the business aspect of their relationship—ergo, him fighting back against the *Calinargo*'s continuing success? He *would* fight. Josh might have sympathised over her father—and telling him had been surprisingly therapeutic—yet there any sentiment ended. Object to the hassle or not, she knew that he would do his utmost to entice customers away from the schooner and on to *his* boat. Yet Abby failed to spot any evidence of change on board the *Hummingbird*.

'Leroy still takes her out in the afternoons?' she had quizzed Vibert.

'Same as usual,' he had confirmed.

'There aren't any. . .improvements?'

'Like them serving chicken casserole?' The black man had grinned. 'No. It's peak period for charters, so my guess is Mr Donner's decided to leave any alterations till later.'

Later? Abby had felt a quiver of unease. The prospect of Josh's retaliation was nerve-racking enough—what form would his counter-attack take?—but the timing had a vital importance. In a few more weeks she and her aunt would be trawling for people to buy the business, and the last thing they could afford was a sudden sag in customer interest *then*.

'How much later?' she had enquired.

'I reckon when things quieten down in two or three months.'

Although Abby would have liked to agree, common sense said that the chances of Josh marking time until the schooner had been sold and she had exited from Grenada were slim. She was responsible for the *Hummingbird*'s reduced fortunes, so he would want to trounce *her*. But when? If only she knew. She clenched her fists in frustration. Once again, she was being forced to play the waiting game.

With her time no longer all-consumed, Abby

also had the opportunity to begin that essential career rethink. An integral part of her success had been her dedication to one or more similar projects. In recent years, she had reliably slogged away at the same kind of illustration until, although she loved to draw, the creative juices had dried up and she had gone stale. The process had become automatic. The zest had disappeared. Now she was hungry for variety, a choice of assignments, the chance to try something different.

'If it's OK with you, I'd like to take the car and visit the Donner boat-yard this morning,' Abby said, the next cruise-free day.

'You're going to see Josh?' her aunt queried, in surprise. Although he had come to the rescue a couple of weeks earlier, Hilda knew that the situation had not changed. The *Calinargo* thrived, the *Hummingbird* went out almost empty—and Josh was not amused. 'Isn't that rather——' She hesitated, choosing between rash, bold and foolish.

'Josh is away on a charter. I'm hoping to see one of his skippers, if he's not out on the ocean, too. He needs some drawings for a book he's written and I thought maybe I could help.'

Her moment of stress gone, the older woman smiled. 'Enjoy yourself.'

An hour later, Abby parked the car beside a blue on white sign announcing 'Donner Marine' and strolled down the ramp. Bathed in sunshine, the boat-yard managed to be both attractive and businesslike. Spread around green manicured lawns, dotted with the pimento, cinnamon and clove trees which give Grenada its nickname of 'Spice Island', she saw a wide range of facilities. There was a dock and a slipway, dinghy storage, a rubbish-disposal unit, showers and toilets, and a small shop which advertised everything from block ice to beer to marine hardware. Boats bobbed beside a jetty, and throughout the area people were engaged in various activities—a hull was being painted, a youth carried provisions, someone lowered a sail. Abby paused to admire the blue anchorage, then headed for a single-storey cabin marked 'Office'.

Knocking on the door, she poked her head inside. 'Excuse me,' she said to a coloured girl who was standing beside a clattering telex machine, 'but would it be possible to speak to Theo?'

'Our big Dane's aboard the *Oz Two*,' the girl told her, and pointed through the window. 'It's moored over there.'

On the deck Abby found a hefty, middle-aged man kneeling over a damaged inflatable. Clad in frayed shorts and a baseball cap, he greeted her with a ready smile.

'So you're the troublemaker the boss keeps complaining about,' he said, when she had introduced herself. Sitting back on his haunches, he admired her slim figure in the amber blouson top and cotton trousers. 'He must be mad!'

Abby laughed. 'I believe you're looking for

someone to provide illustrations for a book and——' she took a folder from beneath her arm and handed over her West Indian drawings '—this is a sample of the work I can produce.'

As he looked through them, Theo gave a low whistle of appreciation. 'You must be a professional?' he said.

'I am,' she acknowledged.

He pursed his lips. 'I don't like to say this, but I think maybe you are too good for me. My book will only appeal to a small market, so the royalties aren't going to be so great,' he explained, in a strong Scandinavian accent.

'It doesn't matter,' Abby assured him. 'What interests me is doing something new.'

Theo grinned. 'In that case, I have the manuscript with me,' he said, climbing to his feet. 'Please, come on board and I'll explain what the publishers want.'

She grasped the massive hand he held out. One tug, and he lifted her on deck. Across the sugar-scoop cockpit, a few steps down, and Abby was sitting in an airy lounge with the manuscript spread out on a table before her.

'The book's written from the chartering slant, and, although its major function is to inform, I also need it to entertain,' he told her. 'My publishers are suggesting little sketches at the beginning and end of each chapter, plus maybe a series of light-hearted cartoons which would depict some of the problems we, as crew, can encounter.'

'What kind of problems?'

Theo rested his elbows on the table. 'Stowage can be a pain in the backside. Most folk bring far too much luggage and it's difficult to store hard suitcases and anything else which is bulky. But we've had blokes turning up with armfuls of tennis rackets and golf clubs and ghetto blasters, and their wives staggering on board weighed down with hair-drying hoods and boxes of wigs. We even had one dame who came complete with ballgown and fur wrap,' he said, shaking a wondering head. 'She thought we dressed for dinner and was afraid the evenings might go cold! Then,' he continued, 'there are the collecting fanatics. They fill the boat with conch shells or pieces of driftwood or coconuts. Another pest is the know-it-all who declares they never burn, spends one day spread-eagled on deck, then the remainder of the trip crouched in their cabin yelling "Don't touch me!"'

Abby grinned. 'Charters aren't just a matter of floating off into the sunset with a light breeze filling the sails and the barometer set for fair?'

'No chance! And even if the clients are good company, and, thank goodness, most of them are, the strain of continuously being close together and on your best behaviour is enormous. You ought to try it.' The Dane sat upright. 'You *should* try it. I can make descriptions, but you'd have a much better idea of what to draw if you went out on a charter yourself. Personal experience is always preferable to learning about something second-hand.'

'True,' she admitted.

'There's a cabin going spare on my next trip,' he said quickly. 'How about it? The boss won't mind.'

Although Abby was not so certain, Josh's views were superfluous. 'Sorry,' she said, 'but I'm tied up with the *Calinargo*.'

'Then why not come the time after that? It's only for a week. Surely you could manage a week off?' he coaxed.

'A week means I'd miss four cruises, and that's too many,' she told him, with a smile. 'I see you've included a section on local dangers such as scorpions and kids trying to sell things and rip-off taxi drivers,' she said, glancing through the sheaf of pages. 'Do you think your publishers would be interested in strips of between four to eight frames for that?'

Theo nodded enthusiastically. 'They're open to any suggestions. Why don't you take the manuscript home and read it, then we can get together again and discuss things in more detail?'

'Will do,' Abby agreed, then hesitated. This was, she had suddenly realised, a chance to do some research into the intriguing question of how his employer had become a chartering mogul with such alacrity. 'The boat-yard seems very extensive—did Josh start it from scratch?' she enquired.

The Dane chuckled. 'He's a go-getter, but I doubt even he could manage that! No, a Canadian guy called Sissons bought the land and built the jetty, dry dock, everything. He'd just started up in business when the political scene in Grenada became hairy and the Americans were asked to intervene. You remember?'

'I read about it in the papers,' she confirmed, recalling the invasion which had made international headlines several years previously.

'Well, not much later Josh happened along with his backpack, and old Sissons wanted out, so——' he shrugged '—they did a deal.'

'Which was to Josh's advantage?' she suggested, with measured casualness.

'Very much so.' The yacht swayed as someone came on deck. 'We have an intruder,' Theo grinned.

'I thought you were repairing this life-raft?' a voice called, and Josh appeared at the top of the steps, a tall, tousle-haired figure in a blue checked shirt and jeans. When he saw Abby he jerked back in visible surprise, then his eyes narrowed. 'What the hell are you doing here?' he demanded, as though she had breached his security and sneaked into the boat-yard on the sly.

'Um. . .hello,' she said weakly.

One minute she had been asking searching questions, and the next the subject under discussion had materialised in living, breathing, highly censorious flesh. Why wasn't he miles away? she wondered. She eyed him curiously. And why, considering that the last time they had met his mood had been easy, did he now seem so resentful of her presence—and almost edgy?

'Don't worry, I haven't come to try and weasel out what you have planned for the *Hummingbird*,' Abby told him pertly.

Theo leaned forward and seemed ready to speak, until Josh's frown silenced him. 'Then you know there's. . .something planned?' he asked haltingly.

'I know you're not going to take what's happened to your trade lying down,' she retorted, and manufactured a smile. 'I await your response with bated breath.'

He frowned at her. 'Mmm,' he said. 'So, what are you up to?' he asked, spreading long brown fingers around either side of the door frame. 'Don't tell me you've decided to go into the charter business and have come to suss out what it takes?'

Abby's gaze travelled around the lounge with its oyster-coloured upholstery, pale-pigmented white beech furniture and Tiffany-style lamps. 'It'd be difficult to compete with anything as splendid as this,' she said wistfully.

'Damn right!' Josh snapped.

'Miss Hammond came to see me, about illustrations for my book,' Theo informed him, clearly determined to mollify.

'You mentioned them,' she said.

'Yes.' Josh massaged his jaw, then stepped down into the cabin. 'Sorry if I seem a bit tense, but——' he bent to stare at something out of the window '—we're having problems with some of our clients.'

Theo looked puzzled. 'Who?' he asked.

'That New York quartet. First they cancel at the last bloody minute when the yacht's been provisioned and we're all standing by, and now they've been in touch to say they've changed their minds and to expect them first thing in the morning.'

'But they were only coming for a week in the first place,' the older man protested.

'They're only coming for three days now!'

'All that way for three days? Won't be much of a holiday.'

'It won't be much of anything,' Josh said drily. 'When they pulled out I told Teresa to take the week off, so she's gone to visit her mother in Trinidad, which means we're now without a cook.'

'Why not try the girl who filled in for us last year?' Theo suggested. 'The meals she prepared weren't all that special, but——'

'After messing us around like this, the New Yorkers don't deserve anything special!' he blasted, then relented. 'We've been in touch and it turns out the girl's heavily pregnant.' He raked an exasperated hand through his hair. 'We've tried everyone.'

The Dane thought for a minute, then he smiled. 'You haven't tried Miss Hammond.'

Josh's eyes swung her way. 'Abby?' he said, in surprise.

'Me?' she croaked.

'Why not? A week away may be too much, but

surely you could squeeze in three days? More informed illustrations would make for a better book,' Theo appealed.

'I don't——' she began.

'You'd be getting us out of a tight spot,' he continued.

'Maybe, but——'

Josh, who had been rubbing at an earlobe in dubious consideration of the idea, now decided that it had merit. 'I did say there might be an occasion when you could help me,' he intruded.

'Ye-es,' Abby agreed reluctantly.

'This is it.'

She spread her hands in supplication. 'But I'm not a cook.'

'You're not a cruise magnate, either, yet you seem to be doing pretty well with the *Calinargo*,' Josh replied pithily. 'Who prepares the chicken casserole?'

'Hilda and I take it in turns.'

'You can serve that for dinner one evening, and surely you could rustle up a few other dishes?'

'Yes, but they'd be nowhere near cordon bleu standard,' Abby protested.

'That's OK,' Josh said dismissively. 'All we need is for them to be halfway edible.'

'You'd get first-hand ideas for the illustrations,' Theo wheedled.

'Plus a chance to sail around the Grenadines and, in what will be ample free time, enjoy some of the most beautiful islands on earth,' Josh added in smiling persuasion.

Abby hesitated—and heard alarm bells ring, loud and long. Theo had talked about the strain of being in close proximity to clients on a charter, but if she agreed to join Josh, how would she cope with being in close proximity to *him*? 'I don't know how anything works on a boat,' she said defensively. 'The only galley I've ever been in is on the *Calinargo*, so——'

'My yachts are high-tech jobs with state of the art facilities which make cooking so-oo simple,' Josh crooned. 'And I solemnly swear that, whenever you call, I'll rush in to help.'

Abby sighed. Every hurdle she erected, he promptly dismantled it. Every time she said no, he altered it into a yes. She nibbled at her lip. Although the intention had been to avoid Josh like the plague, she supposed she did owe him a favour—and Hilda and the girls would have no difficulty managing on the two cruises she missed.

'Who are these people from New York?' she enquired.

'Nobody grand,' he hastened to assure her. 'Just two couples with an interest in photography. They've told us they'll be bringing cameras on board, so I imagine they could be bird-watchers or flora and fauna enthusiasts or maybe the kind who spend every nightfall waiting to capture the Green Flash.'

'That's when the last bit of sun disappears into the sea and it shows bright green?' Abby checked, and he nodded. 'Have you seen it?'

'No. I always seem to blink at the crucial moment.'

'I have,' Theo said. 'Binoculars help,' he told her confidentially.

Josh raised a brow. 'So do several gin and tonics.'

'Could be,' the older man laughed, then turned to Abby. 'Will you act as cook?' he implored.

She sighed. 'All right.'

'Good kid!' he exclaimed.

Josh looked at her, his blue eyes serious. 'Thank you,' he said.

'Just pray I don't poison anyone,' Abby said drily.

'I'll take out extra insurance,' he grinned. 'Look, I'm sorry to drop you into the middle of this, but do you think you could give me some idea of menus now so that I can arrange to have the necessary provisions brought on board?'

She nodded. 'How many will there be to feed?'

'Eight. That's the four passengers, plus you, me and two young German guys who crew.'

Theo gathered up his manuscript. 'How'd it be if I put this on Josh's charter and you can read it while you're afloat?' he suggested.

'Good idea,' Abby agreed.

'Is it all right if I hang on to your drawings?' he asked. 'I'm flying over to see my publishers tomorrow and I'd like to show them the quality of work they can expect.'

'Be my guest.'

'Thanks,' the Dane smiled and, after shaking her hand, he disappeared up on deck..

Planning the meals involved making lists, and altering them, and making lists again, but eventually they were complete—as far as they could be. Next, Josh walked her along the jetty to show her the yacht they would be using.

'*Oz Six*.' Abby read the name emblazoned on the hull. 'Are all your boats called Oz something or other?'

''Fraid so,' he said with a lop-sided grin. 'I know it's corny, but it's easy to remember, it fixes Donner Marine as being Aussie-owned, and it reminds me of my roots.'

'Do you miss Australia?'

Josh grimaced. 'Not as much as I did.'

'Presumably you visit from time to time?' she asked as they went on board.

'I've been once. My folks used to come and see me here, but last year I went over for a couple of months and I'm intending to go again next summer.'

'You were in Grenada for—what—five years before you went home?' Abby said, in surprise.

His face took on a shuttered look. 'That's right.' Josh gestured for her to follow him down the steps which lead from the cockpit into the front section of the boat. 'This is the clients' living area,' he explained, as they entered a spacious lounge, 'and here——' he walked ahead down a short corridor, opening doors '—are four double passenger cabins.'

There were glimpses of pastel carpets, beds with satin coverlets, floral-tiled bathrooms; then she needed to retrace her steps in order to go with him into the rear section. Here the lay-out consisted of a dining-room with wrap-around windows, the galley, and beyond it one cabin with twin bunks and two single cabins with beds and private showering facilities. Everywhere the décor was pale and elegant. Everywhere the furnishings and fittings were of the finest quality.

'What do you think?' Josh asked, as they returned to the galley.

Abby's eyes wandered across the fridges and freezer, the shiny modern oven, the yellow and white units with their built-in wine cellar, fitted glassware storage and sea-safe cutlery drawers.

'I think that if I can't produce at least three-star meals from these five-star facilities I should be shot at sunrise!'

He laughed. 'I'm grateful for your helping us out,' he said, and a brow arched. 'I'd give you a hug, only I'm afraid you might throw something at me.'

'If I did I wouldn't miss this time,' Abby retorted, and strode back up on deck. 'When do you want me to report in the morning?' she asked.

'Nine o'clock, please. I'd like us to be on the move before ten.'

She nodded. 'Until tomorrow.'

The next morning, the Ford refused to start. The engine ticked over once, twice, and then died.

'It's never caused any trouble before,' Hilda fretted, as Abby turned the key again and again.

'Perhaps it's a sign that I'm not meant to go.'

'You must! It's good that you can help Josh. It—well, it means we aren't enemies.'

'Does it?' She climbed out of the car. 'I'd better ring for a taxi.'

A taxi was summoned. Abby waited the promised ten minutes and more. The taxi failed to appear. In a fit of desperation, she went out and tried again. Annoyingly, wondrously, the engine roared into life.

By the time she arrived at the boat-yard, it had gone nine-thirty. A holdall in each hand, Abby jogged down towards the yacht. Josh was on deck talking to a group of people, but when he saw her he excused himself and came over.

'I apologise for being so late,' she gabbled, for his face was stern and his mouth tight. 'It was the car. It——'

'Don't worry about it,' he said, lifting her bags on board.

Abby shot him a look. 'Then what are *you* worrying about?' she enquired.

'It's this New York crowd,' he said, as he followed her into the galley. 'They're not two couples—it's a man and three girls.'

'So?'

'There's something fishy about them. For a start, although they're on vacation together they don't appear to know each other all that well.

Then, where most people come to the Caribbean to unwind, they seem. . .poised for action.' He expelled a troubled breath. 'I reckon they've chartered the yacht for another purpose.'

CHAPTER FIVE

'LIKE what?' Abby asked.

Josh frowned. 'I haven't worked that out, but—call it sixth sense—I know they're not your regular tourists.'

'Instead of bird-watchers you could be skippering a boatload of gun-runners?' she suggested.

'If I thought that I wouldn't move an inch from this jetty!'

'Spoilsport,' Abby said, her grey eyes dancing. 'A spot of smuggling on the high seas would make for some interesting cartoons.'

'*Too* interesting. What have you got in these?' he demanded, as he put down her holdalls. 'They weigh a ton.'

'Some extra fruit, vegetables and spices. I went through the menus with my aunt and she suggested variations which'll make the meals jazzier and more Caribbean.

'Five-star?'

'Four—fingers crossed. Hi,' she grinned, when a fair-haired youth peered in.

'Abby, meet Klaus, and this other nosey individual is his brother, Karl,' Josh added, as a second flaxen head appeared. 'As sharks can smell blood from a kilometre away, so these guys' extrasensory perception enables them to detect the presence of young and shapely females.'

'Nice to have you on board,' the boys told her, unabashed.

'Before you unpack, how about saying hello to our passengers?' Josh suggested, when, after some light-hearted banter, the young Germans had departed. 'Gun-runners or not, we are,' he said drily, 'supposed to be one big happy family.'

Up on deck, a chunky, moustachioed man in his forties was taking zoom-lens shots of a nearby islet, while two brunettes and a redhead were draped around on cushions sunning themselves. Abby's eyes opened wide. Going sailing, most women went casual—she wore a simple shirt and shorts, and had tied her hair back into a practical plait—but these girls made no concessions. Each sported fastidiously arranged 'wild' tresses, false eyelashes and energetically applied make-up. Their fingernails were long and lacquered, and from their ears and around their necks hung glittering baubles and beads. It was true they wore bikinis, yet these were minuscule satin affairs which came under the glamour-puss heading and were totally unsuited for messing about in boats.

'I'd like to introduce Abby. She'll be doing the cooking,' Josh explained.

'My name's Sidonie,' said the redhead, a heavy-jawed girl with aggressively plucked eyebrows. Swinging an arm loaded with so many bangles they constituted luggage, she indicated her companions. 'And these are Saskia and Ailish.'

'Hello,' they chorused.

The man broke off from his photography. 'I'm Rod.' He smiled at her. He frowned at the girls. 'I'd be grateful if you'd serve these three small portions. Remember tummy bulges,' he said, when cries of protest erupted.

'Whatever you wish,' Abby promised, though she thought it strange that a man who was decidedly overweight himself should presume to lay down dietary rules for others.

The redhead pushed herself upright and sauntered over to Josh. 'I'm the one your office decided was a fella,' she announced. She looked at him from beneath black spokes of lashes. 'Some mistake.'

And how! Abby thought. Sidonie was a generously proportioned young lady and, with shoulders pulled back, was emphasising a bosom which had to be forty inches plus.

Determinedly ignoring the display, Josh acknowledged that two couples had been expected. 'Are any of you. . .linked?' he enquired.

'Linked?' The redhead shot a horrified glance in Rod's direction. 'You must be joking!'

'We just work together,' the older man told him briefly.

One of the brunettes giggled. 'Yeah. We're business associates.'

'Are you linked to anyone?' Sidonie asked, moving closer to Josh.

He took a hasty step backwards. 'No.'

'So you're available?'

'Er. . .' His reply was a long time coming. 'I guess. What I mean is——'

A predatory glint gleamed in her eyes. 'You're so cute you make my fillings ache,' she pronounced in a breathy, nasal voice. 'I just love tall, dark men.'

'How nice,' he muttered, and retreated some more.

A smile tugged at Abby's lips. Up until now it had seemed as though little could disturb Josh's composure, but this heavy-duty flirting was unsettling him. It was obvious that he had no wish to offend his client, yet if he withdrew any further he would be over the side and into the water. As she recalled his flair for unsettling *her*, she grinned. The biter bit! she thought.

'Dark-haired men with blue eyes?' Abby asked, unable to resist boosting the conversation—and his unease.

Sidonie advanced on him again. 'The bluer the better.'

'You like athletic types, too?' she asked, and was rewarded by his furious look.

When working on the yacht prior to departure, Josh had shed his shirt, so that all he wore was a pair of brief shorts. Deeply tanned and with whorls of black hair on his chest, he had the strong, healthy look of an outdoors man.

'I adore bodies with beautiful muscle tone,' the redhead proclaimed, and slithered covetous fingers around his shoulder.

For a split second Josh froze, then he flashed a

plastic smile. 'It's time we made a start,' he said, and with a hasty sideways swoop he extracted himself and fled back to the safety of the cockpit.

'What do you have lined up for lunch, Abby?' Rod asked pleasantly.

'Soup, followed by shrimp salad and mango mousse,' she informed him.

'Sounds great.'

'I hope so.' She grinned and, with a nod of farewell, she followed Josh.

'All mouth, aren't you?' he hissed, as she appeared.

Abby opened innocent eyes. 'Me?'

'I suppose you think encouraging that Sidonie female is funny?' he demanded, as he checked the fuel gauge and went through his start-up procedure.

Her mouth tweaked. 'I was under the impression she didn't need any encouragement.'

'Too right,' he muttered. 'I've heard of the liberated woman, but——' Words failed him.

'You prefer us to be constrained by convention?' Abby enquired.

'Shackled!'

'How old-fashioned. All the poor creature wants to do is hold your tiny hand in hers.'

'You reckon?' Josh glowered. 'From the moment she stepped on board, that so-called poor creature's been giving me the come-on with a capital C.'

'These days it's called playfully connecting with

another person to let them know you're interested.' Abby grinned. 'You can take classes for it in America.'

'Thank you for that fascinating piece of information,' he said drily.

'My pleasure. You know what the problem is?' she enquired.

'Tell me.'

'It's your sexuality. It's playing havoc with her peace of mind,' Abby announced, and with her plait swinging jauntily down her back she went below.

As she dealt first with the food and later put her clothes away, the *Oz Six* set sail. Collecting up Hilda's recipes, Abby returned to the galley. What lived where in the cupboards was checked, and then she experimented with the various knobs and functions of the cooker. She was formulating a plan of action for the forthcoming meal, when Josh strode rapidly through and disappeared into his cabin.

'What time would you like me to serve lunch?' she asked, when he emerged.

'One-ish, please. By then we'll be moored in a bay towards the north of Grenada,' he explained.

'Do clients and crew eat together?'

'Usually, though. . .' He sighed. 'I guess so.'

'You're frightened of getting sunburned?' Abby suggested, as he thrust first one impatient arm and then the other into a long-sleeved shirt.

'I'm scared witless of being molested,' he said darkly.

'Sidonie's still making chase?'

'She is, and kindly stop laughing. She paid her money to hire my yacht, not me. I hate pushy women,' Josh grumbled.

'After lunch I'm going to suggest we all have a game of Pass the Peanut Just Using Your Body,' Abby said ingenuously.

'Just you try it!' He made an ineffectual attempt to shrug the shirt on to his shoulders. 'What's the matter with this thing?' he demanded.

'One of the sleeves is inside out. Wait,' she warned, when, in wrestling for freedom, he began twisting himself up even tighter.

Abby stepped forward and drew the garment from him, but as she did the breath seemed to catch in her throat. Although Josh had been bare-chested before, it felt as if she were newly and alarmingly revealing his body. She stood rigid. All she could focus on was the breadth of his shoulders, the brown length of his back, the sheen of his skin.

He glanced back. 'OK?' he asked.

Snapping to life, she straightened the shirt and held it out for him. 'Your armour awaits, oh, cowardly one.'

Josh pushed in his arms, drew the collar around his throat, and turned. 'It feels good being dressed by a woman,' he murmured, his blue eyes locking on hers. 'Though it'd feel even better being *un*dressed.'

Abby's heart thumped *fortissimo*. 'You want

me to call Sidonie?' she enquired, as flippantly as she could.

'I want you to fasten my cuffs,' Josh instructed, and held out his wrists to her like a husband of long standing.

'The girls have some exotic names,' she commented as she dealt swiftly with the buttons. She stepped back. 'Do you think they're for real?'

'I doubt it—as I doubt that they're cruising simply for the fun of it.'

'Perhaps they're in show-business and have come to collect a tan?' Abby suggested.

'It'd be far cheaper to stay home and use sunbeds, but you're right,' Josh said cryptically, 'they are in show-business. The minute we cast off, they proceeded to cast off the tops of their bikinis and strut around the deck. An event which caused severe eyestrain on a number of adjacent vessels and a great deal of fighting over the binoculars,' he said, his tone crisp with disapproval. 'Two guys even sailed alongside us for the first half-hour.'

'Shock, horror! Thunder-clap!' Abby exclaimed. 'I know it doesn't happen so much here, but women have been known to strip at hot-spots in Europe—and presumably in Australia?'

'There's stripping and stripping,' Josh rejoined, staying determinedly disgruntled. 'If it's done with a degree of decorum, fine. But that trio are downright posers. They're continually on the move, so everywhere you look you're confronted by naked breasts. They've removed all the mystery,' he complained. 'Hell, there are breasts everywhere!'

She grinned. 'You've said that twice.'

'I know. I can't seem to get past it. Karl and Klaus are no slouches when it comes to ogling the female form, but even they seem shell-shocked.'

'Maybe the *femmes fatales* are naturists.'

'You think so?'

'No,' she had to admit.

Josh shovelled handfuls of shirt into his shorts. 'Our guests'll be needing something to drink. You wouldn't like to enquire what they want, would you?'

'As part of my duties, or to save you from being violated?' Abby asked, laughing, and sped off without waiting for an answer.

Ice-cool colas and fruit juices were requested, and later, as they moored, she served glasses of chilled white wine, the same vintage also being offered with lunch. To her delight the meal went smoothly and she reaped a harvest of compliments, especially from Rod.

'I've had callaloo soup before, but it was never as tasty as that,' he praised.

'What is callaloo?' Sidonie queried, clasping Josh's arm to gain his attention.

'It's the leaf of the dasheen plant,' he explained. 'A local variation on spinach.'

The redhead wrinkled her nose. 'Spinach? You mean that stuff Popeye used to eat?'

'The same,' he said shortly.

Although Josh had given a sigh of relief when the three girls had covered themselves up before arriving at the table, his expression had become noticeably hounded when Sidonie had insisted that he must sit next to her. And, as the meal had progressed, his discomfort had grown. Bad enough that the redhead's wooing had all the finesse of a heavy board, but she was also a compulsive 'toucher'. Abby had watched the pats and elbow nudges with disbelief. Surely the girl must see how Josh recoiled? Couldn't she sense his distaste? Apparently not. But, like the brunettes, Sidonie was a trifle dim.

Although the conversation over lunch had ranged from the German boys' talk of how they were drop-outs from the rat-race, to descriptions of the privately owned islands which dotted the Caribbean, to a series of hilarious anecdotes Rod had told about New York life—the girls had nothing to contribute. The only topic which interested them was their own appearance.

'I think maybe I should apply another frosting of lacquer,' Sidonie brooded, gazing at her fingernails.

Ailish suddenly became animated. 'Why not try that Oriental Sunrise Pink?'

'Be careful it doesn't clash with your lipstick,' Saskia warned.

'Why don't you three go and freshen up?' Rod suggested, his voice flattened by impatience, and there was a palpable sense of release when his companions retreated to their cabins. 'Any chance of our going ashore?' he asked Josh.

'Where?' He frowned out at the nearby coastline. 'Here?'

The older man upended the wine bottle into his glass. 'I wondered about Isle de Ronde? I understand it's a few miles north of Grenada and I read somewhere that there are just a handful of residents who live at one end. I thought that if we moored at the other it'd give us some privacy.'

'Too rolling,' came the summary rejection. Josh rose from the table. 'I'll find us another place. Somewhere calm.'

The lunch table was cleared and the yacht set sail across the sunlit sea. As she washed up, Abby glimpsed green islets and rocky outcrops thick with nesting sea birds. In time they reached a long finger of land where coconut palms waved leisurely heads and the sand gleamed golden, and here the anchor was dropped. By now she had time to spare, so she changed into her swimsuit, found Theo's manuscript, and went up on deck.

'We're off to investigate,' Rod told her, gesturing to where Josh and the boys were helping the girls clamber aboard a small dinghy. 'You won't be coming ashore?'

Conscious that he was verifying her plans and not offering an invitation, Abby shook her head—though as a member of the crew she had not expected to join them.

'You look as if you'll be taking lots of photographs,' she remarked, as he hoisted a large canvas bag packed with cameras and ancillary equipment on to his shoulder.

'Given the chance,' he said.

She watched as the group were ferried to the land then, as they disappeared and as Josh and the boys attended to various duties, she sat down cross-legged among the cushions and lifted the manuscript. Even for someone with a minimal knowledge of sailing it was easy to read, and she had begun the second chapter when Josh suddenly spoke.

'What do you make of that?' he asked.

Startled, Abby looked up. When she read, her concentration was such that whatever else was happening around her ceased to exist, and now she was surprised to find him standing beside her, while Karl and Klaus were in the prow taking turns at diving into the sea.

'It's good.' She grinned. 'Theo's——'

'I'm referring to Rod's behaviour,' he said. 'First the guy asks if we can stop at the empty end of Isle de Ronde, and now——' Josh stared across the water, his eyes reduced to slits by the glare of the sun '—now he's rushed on to an uninhabited island as though it contains everything he needs from life.'

'Well?'

He sighed, as though lumbered with a slow-witted child. 'Doesn't his desire to avoid contact with the rest of the world strike you as peculiar?'

'On the contrary. After New York I would

imagine that to hear nothing but the lap of the surf makes a welcome change.'

'So you reckon he's legit?'

Abby nodded. 'I agree their party's a weird mix, but maybe they happened to be together one night and got a bit merry and someone suggested a Caribbean cruise?'

'Which seemed like a good idea at the time? Could be,' Josh acknowledged reluctantly. 'Rod went through a bottle of wine all by himself at lunch, so clearly he's fond of a drink.'

'Perhaps the earlier cancellation could've been his having doubts,' she suggested.

'Until pressure was brought to bear? It's possible.'

'I assume your rejection of Isle de Ronde was deliberate?' Abby enquired.

He nodded. 'I felt I'd rather it was me who called the shots.'

'Come on, Josh,' she protested. 'You accused me of having an over-active imagination on the *Calinargo*, but aren't you imagining things now?'

'Maybe,' he admitted. 'I guess their being flash doesn't make them suspect.'

'It's only the girls who are flash,' Abby said. 'Rod's a different type.'

'A real barrel of laughs,' Josh said drily.

'He is! He's nice.'

There was silence.

'The girls could be a cover-up,' he muttered.

Abby gave a moan of exasperation. 'For what?' she demanded.

'I don't know. You're the ideas whizz, you tell me.' He straightened. 'I'm going below. One of the passenger cabin doors is sticking and it needs attention.'

Alone again, Abby returned to the manuscript. She read another chapter, and yawned. The hypnotic roll of the boat and the heat of the sun were making her drowsy. She rubbed on tanning cream, then rearranged the cushions, stretched out and closed her eyes.

'Josh!' Through the fog of sleep Abby heard a voice calling, a voice she recognised as Sidonie's. 'Josh, please!' He's working on the door, she thought hazily. Can't you hear his drill? 'Josh!' the appeal came again, this time accompanied by some splashing.

Abby raised her head and fumbled for her sunglasses. Bleary-eyed, she gazed at the sparkling ocean. No sign of the vacuous vamp, or anyone else for that matter. Vaguely she recalled that Karl and Klaus had abandoned their diving and rowed off somewhere in the dinghy. Jettisoning the glasses, Abby slumped back.

'I have a cramp!' Sidonie yelled in a voice like a fog-horn, and it suddenly registered that her cries were coming from the other side of the boat.

Stumbling to her feet, Abby lurched across the deck. She blinked. She rubbed her eyes. A few yards away, she saw Sidonie in the water. Her back towards her, the redhead was flinging out her arms in circles and thrashing wildly. Oh, no, she was drowning!

'Josh?'

The appeal came again—and so did the drone of the drill. *She* would need to go to the rescue, Abby realised fuzzily. Now. There was not a moment to waste. Clambering over the restraining wire, she half jumped, half fell into the sea. The water was colder than she had imagined and the shock shuddered through her body, jolting her awake.

'I'm coming,' she gasped as she surfaced, though it was doubtful that Sidonie would hear over her splashing.

As Abby struck out, she tried desperately to remember the life-saving practice she had been taught at school. Didn't you calm the victim, then take hold of them under the arms and, swimming on your back, keep their head above water? And, if they grabbed and seemed liable to pull you down, weren't you supposed to knock them out cold? Dubiously she thought of Sidonie's truck-driver chin. Could she manage that?

'I'm here,' she gasped, arriving alongside. 'Now, please——'

Clunk! A flung-out arm struck her on the brow. This is the wrong way round, Abby thought in the split second before the arm slithered over her head and forced her beneath the waves. Caught with her mouth open and half-stunned, she swallowed what seemed like gallons of salt water.

'Keep calm,' she appealed, spluttering red-faced to the surface, but the arm seemed to have become attached to the back of her head, and as

Sidonie flailed she found herself going under again.

Kicking valiantly, Abby made her way up, managed one gulp of air, and was immediately pressed down underwater. She must break free, she realised, but when she attempted to swim away a sharp pain seared at the nape of her neck and she was jerked back. Something had become tangled up in her hair. Somehow she was trapped. In an attempt to make the redhead aware of the problem, she reached blindly for her—and was thrust off.

Abby ordered herself to think. It was vital that she calm Sidonie and keep calm herself. But it was also vital that she breathe. Her lungs were bursting. Her eyes stung. Twisting her head, she fought to release herself, but again the pain ripped. What could she do? How did she get free? She had to breathe. She must. She *must*.

Suddenly, two hands caught at her waist and Abby found herself being raised up into sweet, blessed, life-bestowing air.

'Hang on to me and keep *still*!' Josh rasped. Was he speaking to her or Sidonie? she wondered, coughing and gasping. The situation was confused. Both of them seemed to be tangled up around him and with each other. 'Abby, are you all right?' she heard him ask, from behind.

'I'm f-fine,' she gurgled, recovering.

'Don't!' he ordered, as she made to turn. 'One of Sidonie's bracelets is hooked into your plait. If you both stay where you are and tread water, I'll try to release it.' She felt his fingers working in her hair. 'Done it,' he muttered at last.

Abby swivelled round. 'Thanks.' She smiled.

'Oh, Josh, if you hadn't seen us and dived in, it's real scary to think what would've happened,' Sidonie gushed, sticking herself on to his shoulder like Superglue.

'All part of the service,' he replied tersely. 'You're sure you're all right?' he asked Abby again, and she nodded.

'She was only under the water for a moment,' the redhead pouted. 'I didn't see her coming and I hit her by mistake. But *I* was the one in trouble—with cramp.'

'Which has gone?' he enquired.

She wiggled her head. 'Almost.'

'Wonderful,' he grated. Swimming in the middle, Josh shepherded them to the yacht. 'Go and dry yourself,' he told Sidonie, when they were back on deck. 'Chill is one of the causes of cramp and I'm sure you wouldn't want to risk it again.'

She gave him a small shove. 'You're so thoughtful,' she said.

'When you saw her in the water why the hell didn't you come for me?' Josh demanded as the redhead disappeared below.

'Because you were busy and Sidonie was drowning,' Abby replied.

'Drowning, and her hair hardly got wet? The woman might be dumber than a box of rocks, but she's also highly innovative!'

Abby lifted her towel and began drying herself. 'She looked as if she was drowning,' she amended. 'Maybe I didn't see her go down the regulation three times, but——'

'You didn't see her go down once, did you?' Josh demanded, the water running down his long, tanned legs to form a puddle at his feet. 'What was she doing, yelling for me?'

Abby flushed. 'Yes.'

'Yet it never crossed your mind that the silly bitch might be putting on an act?' he countered, his fury making it plain that where bitches were concerned *she* was the silliest.

'I'd been asleep, and I woke up suddenly, and—and I did what anyone else would have done. Sidonie is your client, and Donner Marine must have a responsibility towards their clients, and, temporarily, I can be classed as an employee of Donner Marine. Though why I ever agreed to come on this boat with you I have no idea!' she flung at him, her resentment at the injustice of his attack growing.

Josh sighed. 'Abby——'

'Sidonie appeared to be in difficulties, and how was I supposed to know otherwise?' she protested. 'And what would the police, or the coroner, or the media, have said if she had drowned and I'd told them I'd stood on deck and done nothing because she was yelling your name and not mine? And how would *I* have felt?'

'Abby——' he said, but again got no further.

'Is that what you expected, me to stand there

and do nothing? It might be your answer, but it's certainly not mine! And although Sidonie reckoned I was under the water just for a moment, it felt like hours, weeks, *years*. I put my life at risk on your behalf! I——'

'Do you think you could give me a signal when you're ready to listen?' he queried. 'Like taking a breath or something?'

'The next time I notice one of your clients thrashing around in the ocean, I shall sit back and read the newspaper—unless they despatch a memo specifically requesting *my* help. In duplicate!' Like a clockwork mechanism, her tirade wound down. 'I'm listening,' Abby informed him.

'I want to apologise for bawling you out just now.'

'Do you?'

'Yes. It's just that when I think of how potentially dangerous that woman's moronic play-acting was——' Josh shuddered and stepped closer. 'Abby,' he said, his fingers caressing the tender flesh on the inside of her elbow, 'there's something I must tell you.' He hesitated. 'I——'

'Decided to be friends again after all that yelling?' a voice broke in, and Sidonie bounced back. Dry now, she had redone her hair, and changed into a low-cut peasant blouse and black footless tights. 'Don't worry, guys,' she smiled. 'I only heard the noise, not the words.'

Josh straightened his shoulders. 'We're more than friends,' he said.

Abby shot him a startled look. 'More?' she asked.

'Much more.' His voice was firm. 'We're linked.'

'Yipes!' the redhead exclaimed. 'I've forgotten my earrings. Be back in a minute.'

'I never realised you were a closet Marx brother,' Abby hissed, as the girl rushed away.

'I'm not,' he protested.

'You damn well are! If you think I'm prepared to go along with some charade which involves——' What it involved was left unsaid. 'I'm prepared to be your cook, but I'm not prepared to be your——'

'Lover? Mistress? My intended?' Josh said, when she dried up again. 'But you must see that this is the ideal opportunity to get Sidonie off my back.'

'You had the opportunity earlier—when she asked if you were available,' Abby reminded him.

'And I blew it. So don't make me pass up a second chance.' He circled the flat of his hand over the damp hair which covered his chest. 'Co-operate, please?'

Abby ripped the band from the end of her pigtail and began hastily unplaiting her hair. She wished he wouldn't look at her like that, with his brows down low and his eyes bluely intent and appealing. And she wished he would not rub his chest. Josh managed to blend little-boy-lost with the sexiest man alive, a combination which did nothing for her equilibrium.

'I came to your rescue just now—couldn't you come to mine?' he asked. 'All I need is the minimal amount of pretence. Abby, you have to help me! If that woman paws me again I swear I'll throw up.'

'You're taking it too seriously. Her flirting's just good knockabout stuff, that's all,' she argued.

He shook his head. 'I'm getting paranoid. Even the thought of her touching me makes me want to suck my thumb and *writhe*.'

She threw him an impatient look. 'How minimal?' she enquired.

'Just a verbal agreement that we're involved.' Josh paused. 'And maybe the occasional affectionate glance.'

Abby jumped through mental hoops. Could she act as his. . .lover? Yes, though she would rather not. Yet he *had* pulled her out of the water, and Sidonie *was* a complete pain.

'OK, we'll tell Sidonie we're dating,' she said.

'Dating?' Josh looked aghast. 'I'm thirty-four and a heterosexual male. I don't go out on "dates".' He phutted out the word like a plum stone. 'I stay in and have relationships.'

'Meaningful ones?' Abby asked drily.

'Always, though I'm talking in the past tense. Very past. But——'

'So we tell her we have a relationship,' she adjusted.

'One which excludes any other woman laying so much as a finger on me,' Josh defined.

'You want bells on this, don't you?' Abby

demanded. 'Hello, Sidonie,' she said, as the girl reappeared on deck. She took a breath, but Josh got there ahead of her.

'Abby and I have decided to come clean,' he announced. 'We think you ought to know that we're involved.' He paused, then added, 'Emotionally and sexually.'

Abby felt a tremor of alarm. At the 'sexually' his voice had throbbed, and now he was hooking an arm around her waist and drawing her against the warm, damp length of his body. She should, she knew, move away, yet regrettably her thoughts failed to translate themselves into action.

The redhead frowned. 'Why didn't you say so earlier?'

'Business etiquette,' he told her cheerfully. 'As two people working together and giving a service to others, we prefer to be discreet. We feel it's unprofessional to impose our private feelings too strongly on others.' He hugged Abby closer. 'Right, sweetheart?' he asked.

'Right,' she heard herself echo lamely.

Brow furrowed, Sidonie mulled over what he had said. 'But you were shouting at each other a few minutes ago,' she muttered sulkily.

'All lovers have tiffs.' He pointed to the shore where Karl and Klaus had returned in the dinghy and were picking up Rod and the other two girls. 'Look, your friends are back.'

The diversion worked.

'Hi, guys!' Sidonie called, and rushed to the side of the boat where she commenced a shouted recital of how she had had a narrow escape from drowning—an escape in which Josh played the role of knight errant and Abby's inclusion was coincidental.

When the group arrived back on board, Abby provided drinks and later went off to shower. The next, and final, stop of the day would be at Carriacou, Grenada's sister isle and the largest of the Grenadine islands, and she spent the short journey preparing the chicken casserole and accompanying dessert.

'You look terrific,' Rod said, grinning, when they anchored in a sheltered bay and she took round the aperitifs which had been ordered earlier.

After a day of being sartorially sensible, Abby had changed into a filmy white jumpsuit trimmed with satin and cinched at the waist with a wide, butter-soft black leather belt. Her eyelids shimmered pale lilac, and her lashes had been brushed with mascara. She did not look as conspicuous as Sidonie and company who, in back-baring get-ups, were not just dressed to the nines, but to the ninety-nine-point-nines, but she considered that she had the edge on elegance.

'Thank you,' she smiled.

Josh strolled from the bow of the yacht. 'She's beautiful,' he said and, taking hold of her chin in proprietorial fingers, he kissed her on the lips.

Caught by surprise, Abby gazed at him. What had happened to a minimal pretence? she wondered. The agreement had been to persuade

Sidonie to drop him from her sphere of attention, not to act out a full-scale romance for Rod's benefit.

The older man frowned. 'Do I take it you two have something going between you?'

'You could put it that way,' Josh said, and shone her a charming, deeply sexual smile. 'In fact——'

Fearful of what he might say next, Abby ransacked her mind for a different—safer—topic. 'Are you a professional photographer?' she asked Rod hurriedly.

He frowned down into his glass. 'Yeah.'

'Any particular speciality?' she enquired.

'I've broadened my range now——' he took a gulp of whisky '—but I used to be in fashion. My photographs have appeared in all the major American women's magazines and some British ones.' He gave a sudden grin. 'I did several assignments for *Vogue*, and on one occasion we went to Bangkok. Is that some city! We——'

His tales of the international shoots he had done were varied and beguiling. When the girls wandered up even they seemed intrigued, and so his escapades dominated the conversation throughout dinner. In due course, coffee was drunk and liqueurs offered, and both the raconteur and the evening gradually wound down.

'Time I hit the sack,' Rod declared, finishing the last in a long line of drinks. He turned to his companions. 'You three need your beauty sleep, too.'

'It's early,' Sidonie grumbled, but, like the other girls, she rose to her feet. 'Goodnight,' she said, her eyes fixing on Josh. All evening she had been subdued. She had not touched him nor tried to flirt, though with him sitting next to Abby at one end of the table while she was parked at the other, there had been little chance. But now, as the redhead strolled past, she trailed her fingertips across the back of his neck. 'Sleep tight,' she purred.

Josh's shoulder muscles stiffened. 'Will do,' he replied.

When the clients had gone, Karl and Klaus helped Abby clear the table and wash up and then went off to bed.

'How about a breath of fresh air before we turn in?' Josh suggested when everything had been stacked away.

Out on deck, Abby gazed around. High in the sky a silver moon shone among a million scattered stars, while on the dark bulk of the island palm trees swayed and lights twinkled in the streets of a small town. The sound of laughter from another moored yacht carried across the water. A fish jumped, plopped, and was gone, leaving behind ever-widening circles. A soft chiffon breeze caressed her skin.

Abby sighed. 'I like the Caribbean.'

Josh reached out and touched her hair. 'I like you,' he said.

Her response was abrupt and indignant. 'Don't

play games. There's no one around, so there's no need for——'

'There's every need,' he murmured, and, placing a hand on either side of her head, he kissed her.

It was an adult kiss of unexpected ferocity. Abby's pulse-rate accelerated. Every nerve-end throbbed. He mustn't do this, it isn't *fair*, a part of her protested. She must stop him. She must step away. But did she want to? Yes. No. For a frantic moment, mind and body tugged in opposite directions, but then, as Josh's hands moved to her shoulders, her heart traitorously connived and she began kissing him back.

The moist, glowing contact of their lips ignited sparks, and, as his tongue probed and stroked, Abby's senses became white-hot. She felt the unbearably soft skin at the back of his bronzed neck, tasted him, breathed in his breath.

'Sweetheart,' he muttered, his hands sliding down to pull her against him so that she was left in no doubt about the urgency of his arousal.

Her breasts tautened. A roar penetrated her skin. Exciting her—and quickly—seemed to be Josh's special area of study. But she felt more than excitement. . .didn't she? Abby had told herself that the attraction he held was purely physical, yet all of a sudden she was no longer sure. To want him so much and for his kisses to seem so *right*, surely something else had to be involved? Was that 'something' her emotions?

'Josh,' she began, not knowing what she

intended to say, but suddenly something moved in the corner of her eye. As her head whipped round, she gave a sharp intake of breath. Sidonie was standing there in the darkness.

Her stomach hollowed. Josh might be as aroused as she, but his kissing had been for a purpose. He had recognised yet another opportunity, and used it—the bastard!

Abby wrenched herself free. 'I'll see you tomorrow, darling,' she snapped, and marched across the deck and down to her cabin.

CHAPTER SIX

AFTER breakfast the next morning, it was agreed that everyone would go ashore. Josh needed to speak to his yard, the German youths hoped to meet up with friends from another boat, and the girls were eager to buy batik sarongs, coral necklaces and palm-frond baskets. Rod and Abby had shorter shopping lists—he wanted a couple of postcards, while she would stock up with fresh bread rolls.

'I guess you'd better get another bottle of whisky,' Josh told her as they left the pier. He looked ahead to where Rod walked along. 'If your photographer friend carries on at his present rate he's in danger of drinking us dry.'

'No problem,' she said briskly, and wheeled off to the grocery shop he had indicated.

Since setting eyes on Josh again, Abby had been brisk. It was the only way. She did not give a damn about saving him from Sidonie; the first—the only—priority was saving herself from him! Yet she must keep things in perspective. All she had to do was get through today and tomorrow in proximity to him, and, although she did not view the prospect with overpowering serenity, it was no reason to fall apart.

The rolls and whisky purchased, Abby wandered along the short stretch of the main street which ran parallel to the beach. Dotted up and down were more shops—she passed one where the girls were examining swimwear—a rum shop, two banks and a tiny museum. Housewives chatted. Old men congregated on corners. Dogs slept in the sun. The pace was West Indian lazy.

Sweat trickling down her back alerted her to the need for a cool drink. In her meanderings, Abby had noticed an open-air bar where scarlet poinsettias bloomed around a flagged terrace, and now she headed back towards it.

'Come and join me,' someone said as she approached, and she saw Rod sitting at an umbrellaed table with a glass of rum punch before him.

'What's happened to your boyfriend?' he enquired, when a waiter had brought the fruit juice she ordered.

'Josh is phoning his yard for an update on his other charters, but he isn't my boyfriend. We're only pretending to be involved. Sidonie has been——' She shot him an awkward smile. Even though he had shown little affection for the redhead, the photographer had accompanied her on holiday. 'Coming on a bit strong,' she completed haltingly.

Rod chuckled. 'And he's running scared? Par for the course, kiddo. I've only worked with her twice, but each time she's pinpointed some poor jerk and done her best to eat them alive.' He leaned across the table. 'The trouble is that some photographs of her appeared in a magazine under the heading of "the scintillating and sublime Sidonie", and now she's convinced that every guy she meets has the hots for her.'

'Sidonie's a model?' Abby said in amazement. Maybe the camera did lie, but surely it could not transform the redhead into a creature of classic beauty?

'Of a sort.' Rod looked down into his drink and then looked up. 'She poses in the nude.'

Cogs spun, gears meshed. 'That's why you're here, isn't it?' Abby said in a sudden flash of understanding. 'That's why you're so keen on unpeopled islands? You're taking photographs for—for a girlie magazine?'

'There's a big market in naked females rolling around in the sand,' he said astringently. 'I guess I should've explained, and I intended to, but Josh seemed sorta critical from the moment we arrived. I didn't want any trouble, so I decided to leave him in ignorance. Shocked?' he bit out.

She frowned, considering. 'More surprised.'

'Not as surprised as I am to find myself involved in this kind of racket. Won't I have some tales to tell my grandchildren!' Rod gave a sour smile. 'But you should hear Sidonie justify her actions. She first took her clothes off, so she reckons, because her life was stagnating and she wanted to do something special. And now she claims the photographs are art. Art!' he said bitterly.

'Why do you do it if it makes you so unhappy?' Abby enquired.

He poured the last inch of punch down his throat. 'It's a long story,' he muttered, and nodded down the street. 'There are Josh and the others. I wonder if they'd like a drink.'

Everyone did. Time slipped by, and when they returned to the yacht Abby went straight into the galley and began assembling a crab and lobster picnic. Their lunch destination was a nearby sandy islet and, after a short detour to top up with fresh water, they sailed over to it. People and food were ferried to a clearing beneath the palms where they dined *alfresco*.

'We're going to snorkel,' Karl announced when the after-lunch siesta had come to an end. 'Anyone care to join us?'

'We carry all the necessary gear,' Josh told his clients, 'and you'll see some exotic fish among the reefs.'

Ailish looked interested. 'How about it?' she asked Rod.

'Another day.' He waited until the German youths had departed, then picked up his bag. 'Come along, girls,' he instructed. 'It's time we took a stroll.'

'I wish I knew what the hell they're up to,' Josh muttered as the quartet walked away. 'Maybe I should follow them?'

Abby's lips curved. 'It'd be an eye-opener if you did.'

'How?'

'Rod's "broadening of his range" means that he now photographs centrefolds. He told me this morning.'

Josh looked at her in astonishment. 'Soft porn?' he exclaimed, and threw back his head and laughed. 'That's great!'

'It is?' she said, bemused by such emphatic delight.

'I'd a damn sight rather he took nude studies than traded in illegal substances!'

Now it was Abby's turn to be astonished. 'You thought Rod was involved in drugs?' she queried.

He nodded. 'The way he constantly hauled that bag around was making me nervous. You remember you mentioned smuggling? Well, I'd begun to wonder whether he might be carrying a radio receiver in order to make contact with a boat, one which would rendezvous and pass over parcels of cocaine, heroin, whatever,' Josh explained. 'Boats are ideal for transacting shady business.'

'He'd have had to take any drugs out through Customs when he left Grenada,' she protested.

'It's a risk these courier guys are prepared to run.' Josh's voice hardened. 'But there's no way I'd allow my yachts to be involved in *that* kind of traffic!' Resting against the palm tree, which provided a back rest, he brooded for a moment. 'The idea of the four of them trotting off to take nude shots is——' he grimaced '—sleazy, but I guess I can't object, so long as they do it away from the yacht and in privacy.'

Abby nodded. 'The girls are over twenty-one and posing is their choice.'

'Some choice!'

'Well, millions of men do choose to buy girlie magazines.' Tilting her head, she grinned. 'You?'

'I must own up to a time in my teens when a well-thumbed copy of *Playboy* resided beneath my bed. Though, naturally, I didn't buy it to indulge my fantasies but in order to read the articles,' Josh told her, deadpan.

'Naturally,' Abby said.

'You've not thought of revealing all for the camera?' he enquired with a lift of mischievous eyebrows.

'Never been asked.'

'Yet.' His eyes moved over her swimsuited figure, lingering on the swell of the golden breasts revealed in the low neckline. 'Sweetheart, you leave those top-heavy bimbos standing. You——'

Abby stiffened. Somewhere along the way her briskness had been discarded and the mood had become relaxed, but now she realised her mistake. 'What did Sidonie have to say last night?' she cut in.

'Not a word. By the time I'd blasted her out for spying on us she was speechless.' Josh's mouth thinned. 'When you turned and I saw her standing there, I felt like murdering the damn woman. However, homicide is not the answer to all of life's little problems, so. . .' He shrugged.

'You—you hadn't realised she was there before?' Abby faltered.

'Of course not.'

She sat up and ran her hands through her hair. 'So now Sidonie realises you're well and truly out of bounds,' she said brightly.

'She should, though I doubt it,' Josh retorted. 'She may have kept her distance today, but I've caught her giving us some very speculative glances. Which could have something to do with the fact that you haven't seemed entirely infatuated,' he added sardonically.

'You want me to treat you like a god?' Abby demanded.

'And indulge my every whim.'

'How about your indulging one of mine?' she asked.

'Anything! Anything!' he declared dramatically.

'Please would you take me back to the yacht? Although there isn't much food left over from lunch, it's time that what there is went back in the cool.'

Josh groaned. 'Yes, ma'am.'

While she had been shopping, Ailish had seen a poster advertising a dance in town that evening, and on reassembling all three girls insisted that they must go.

'If you do there won't be time to cruise any further,' Josh warned.

'That's OK,' Rod said.

'And the dance'll be a homespun, small-scale affair,' he explained, but decisions were already being made as to what to wear.

'How about joining us?' Sidonie asked him.

'I have things to do,' Josh said quickly.

'No, thanks,' Rod and Abby joined in, though the redhead had yet to get around to inviting them.

'How about you two?' she enquired, smiling at the German boys.

Karl shrugged. 'OK.'

'OK,' echoed Klaus.

The *Oz Six* returned to its earlier anchorage and, as Sidonie and company went off to begin zealous dressing, face-painting and hair-arranging, Abby made dinner. The menu was pumpkin soup, followed by baked fish and a tropical fruit crumble, yet although the food was good, the girls wolfed down their meals so quickly that they could not have tasted a thing.

'Let's go,' the redhead said the moment dessert had been eaten, and in a dazzle of day-glo boob-tubes and lurex skirts her confederates started up from the table. 'March!' she instructed Karl and Klaus.

They marched, and the five of them piled into the dinghy.

'Carriacou doesn't know what's about to hit it,' Josh remarked drolly, as the sound of the out-board faded into the distance.

Not much later, Abby was making a fresh pot of coffee in the galley when she heard the put-put of an approaching engine. What had been forgotten? she wondered. Hair lacquer? Lipstick? A perfume spray? But it turned out that the owner of another charter yacht had spotted the *Oz Six* and come over.

'You must join me for a drink,' she heard him say when Josh went to investigate. 'It's ages since we've managed to get together.'

'Months,' he agreed, and came back to poke his head into the galley. 'OK if I disappear for an hour?' he asked.

Abby smiled. 'Do.'

Back at the dinner table, Rod was helping himself to another shot of malt whisky. 'So we're alone,' he said.

She nodded. 'More coffee?'

He hooked his hand around his glass. 'I'll stick with this, thanks. You've told Josh why the girls and I are here?' he demanded, a touch querulously.

'Yes.'

'Well, now you can tell him that we've finished the shoot, so there's no reason for him to feel compromised.' Rod took a gulp of whisky. 'You don't throw stones, do you, Abby?' he said suddenly.

'I beg your pardon?'

'My wife does, and my kids. Not that I see much of my family these days. Divorced,' he mumbled. 'Badly.'

His forlorn tone tugged at her heart-strings. 'I'm sorry,' she said gently.

'I knew you would be.' For a minute or two, he stared into his glass, then he revived. 'About the stones. What I mean is, Abby, when I told you the line I was in you didn't criticise, you didn't rant and rave, you realised that I have no choice.' His arm came out like the arm of a crane, and his fingers fastened around her wrist. 'You're a wonderful girl, Abby. You don't despise me.'

She frowned. Although the photographer's alcohol consumption had been consistently high it had not appeared to affect him, but now his words were slurred.

'Rod——' she began, attempting to ease her hand away.

'I knew we were kindred souls the moment I set eyes on you, Abby. You think I'm a swell guy, don't you, Abby?' he said, using her name as if it was cement which bonded her to him. 'My wife doesn't. She reckons I drink too much.' He released her and poured himself another slug, the whisky splashing up the inside of the glass. 'You don't think that, do you, Abby?' he asked, looking at her out of plaintive brown eyes.

'I think you'd be wise to cut down a little,' she said.

'See the difference?' Rod enquired of some unseen audience. 'You suggest I cut down, whereas my wife demands total absti——' he fumbled over the pronunciation '—abstinence. She claims it's my fault I'm no longer doing fashion pics. So I had a few drinks and missed the occasional appointment, but when a guy's away from home he needs some relaxation. What she doesn't realise is that photography's a cut-throat business. Open the door an inch and some younger guy's through it punching and kicking you to a pulp.' He rested his chin on his hand and smiled at her. 'You'd never kick a man when he's down, Abby.'

'I must do the washing-up,' she announced, impatient of his maudlin adoration, and began to clear the table.

Rod staggered to his feet. 'We'll do it together.'

'No, thanks. You're the client, and Josh'd be furious if he knew I'd let you help,' Abby insisted, as he clattered one plate on top of another. 'Please.'

'OK.' He reached for the whisky bottle again. 'But Josh won't mind if I come and talk to you.'

Josh might not have minded, but as Abby tackled the pots the photographer's presence became increasingly oppressive. With avid use of her name, he embarked on a self-pitying recital which wove an unsteady path around her imagined virtues, his wife's sins and his loneliness. It was a sad tale and she sympathised, yet by the time he had finished blaming everyone else for his misfortunes she also felt like giving him a good shake.

'If I were you I'd go back to New York and enrol with Alcoholics Anonymous, or whatever self-help group operates there,' Abby declared when he'd lumbered to a halt.

'I agree with everything you say,' he muttered,

forgetting that his idol was echoing a suggestion which his wife—the villainess—had been advocating for years. As she finished the drying-up, Rod set down his glass and, without warning, lunged and grabbed so that Abby was banged breathlessly up against him. 'We must get together like this more often,' he chuckled.

She gave a silent groan. The pity-me stage, it appeared, was over and now his libido was asserting itself.

'Why don't you go and lie down?' she suggested, extricating herself.

'I will, if you'll come with me.'

'No, thanks,' she said crisply.

A leaden arm landed around her shoulders. 'Is it because I'm older than you?' Rod enquired. He rubbed his face against hers, his moustache scratching her cheek. 'Older men have a lot going for them.'

'It's because I'm not interested!' Abby replied, and gave an almighty heave which sent him staggering back.

'Josh won't mind,' he bubbled. 'You said he wasn't your boyfriend, so——'

'He is now,' she announced, in the hope of deflecting him. 'The attraction's always been there, and last night it suddenly erupted.'

He blinked bloodshot eyes. 'I don't believe you.'

'Too bad,' she said pertly. 'However, whether you do or not it doesn't matter because I'm going to bed.'

'But it's only the middle of the evening.'

'Goodnight!'

In her cabin, Abby sat on the bed and sighed. Apart from the early hour and being wide awake, she had no hope of sleep with Rod moving around. He was not a threat, just a pest—though with the door locked she was safe anyway—but his drunken lurchings were making the yacht roll. If only *he* would go to bed—but the clink of glass on glass warned that he was seeking solace in yet another drink. Noticing Theo's manuscript, she picked it up and tried to read, but it was no use. She put away some clothes, pulled a face at herself in the mirror, and sat down on the bed again. Suddenly, she tensed. The sway of the boat and soft crashes along the corridor gave notice of Rod's approach.

He knocked on the door. 'Abby,' he called, 'I know you're not asleep. Abby, I know what you're thinking. I understand your doubts, but you and I are meant to be. It's karma. It's our destiny.'

She raised despairing eyes to the ceiling. Not only was the idea cock-eyed, but every word he uttered sounded like something from a third-rate film.

'You mustn't fight it,' Rod said.

Abby sat tight. Go away! she ordered him silently, and eventually he did. She heard him pour himself a further drink, then stagger out across the cockpit and into the passengers' quarters. All went still. She waited a few minutes, then quietly opened the door and tiptoed along to the dining-room. Although Rod appeared to have retired for the night, it seemed prudent to remove the alcohol supply—just in case.

Lifting the liqueurs tray, she took it through to the galley and stashed the bottles away. She locked the cupboard and pocketed the key. She was giving herself a mental pat on the back for foresight, when the boat rocked, footsteps padded, and a figure loomed in the doorway.

'Oh!' she gasped, her hand flying to her throat, but then she laughed. 'It's you!' she said, grinning at Josh. 'Had a good time?'

'Yes, thanks.'

'I was so busy putting the booze away I didn't hear you return. Rod's been tossing back the whiskies,' she explained as he joined her, 'so I decided to stem the flow.'

Josh frowned. 'The guy's stoned?'

''Fraid so.'

'Has he been giving you trouble?'

'No.' She hesitated. 'Not really.'

'And what's that supposed to mean?' he demanded.

'It means he's been a bit of a nuisance, but I can handle him.' Abby sighed. 'He was telling me about the bad divorce he'd been through and how his wife——'

'Doesn't understand him?' Josh cut in.

'More or less.'

'And you fell for it?'

'There was nothing to fall for,' she defended,

seeing shades of how she had erroneously believed Sidonie to be drowning. 'The situation may be hackneyed, but the man does have his troubles.'

'The man, who has been lusting after you ever since we set sail, can recognise a soft heart when he sees one,' Josh told her pungently. He walked towards the filter machine. 'I'm going to have some coffee. Want some?'

'Please.'

'All divorces are bad,' he remarked as, with steaming mugs in hand, they went into the dining-room. He sat down to face her across the table. 'Even with those which are highly civilised, there's always some poor devil who suffers.'

Abby recognised the grim voice of experience. 'You?' she said. Josh nodded. 'How long were you married?'

'Two years, that's all, but then it took me five to exorcise the ghost of the divorce.'

'Which is why you didn't go back to Australia?'

'Yup. I felt I'd messed up Sarah's—my ex-wife's—life, and I wasn't too proud of myself.' He gave a wry laugh. 'Is that some understatement! The truth is I couldn't bring myself to face up to either my own failings or the woman I thought I'd ruined.' He took a mouthful of coffee. 'You've heard one sob story tonight—are you willing to hear another?'

She smiled. 'Fire away.'

Stretching back in his chair, Josh linked his hands behind his head. 'Sarah and I grew up in the same neighbourhood, went to the same school, and were married just after I qualified,' he said slowly. 'She worked for a year—she was a secretary with a television company—then she announced that she wanted to stay home and have babies. I didn't agree.'

'You don't like kids?' Abby enquired.

'I do, but——' He sighed. 'Although I'd landed a good job with a top-notch legal firm and my career seemed set, basically I'd gone into law because my father and my grandfather had been lawyers and it was what was expected of me. I'd had doubts at college about whether I was doing the right thing and ignored them, but working crystallised my thoughts and eventually I was forced to admit that I'd made the wrong choice. At which point I broke out into a cold sweat.' Josh grimaced as the memories came back. 'I'd spent years training to be a damn lawyer and my folks were delighted, and——' He sighed again. 'I told Sarah that I wanted to pack in my job and look for something else, but when she asked what that somehing was, I couldn't tell her—I genuinely had no idea—and, for some reason, she decided that the whole thing was an excuse to avoid having a family. I told her she was nuts, that all I wanted was to postpone a child until I'd sorted out my future, but she wouldn't listen.'

'How old were you both?'

'I was twenty-seven and Sarah would've been twenty-five.'

'Twenty-five isn't ancient. Good grief, that's

my age. Surely she could have agreed to postpone children, too?'

'To me it seemed a reasonable request, but she said the whole point in getting married was to have kids and she wanted them now. That hurt—I thought she'd married me for me,' he said ruefully. 'However, I was given an ultimatum: either we have a child or we divorce. I tried again to plead my case, but it was no go.' Josh swigged at his coffee. 'Sarah was a great girl for dissecting everything, and the next day she announced that, as I'd become a lawyer because it was what was expected, so it was now clear that we'd married for the same reason. At the time I disagreed, though now I reckon she was right,' he said wryly. 'Our families had been friends for years, and there was always this subliminal hope that we'd join up,' he explained.

Abby looked at him over the rim of her mug. 'Then came the civilised divorce?'

He nodded. 'We were both so polite. No one wept. No one shouted. We just said goodbye and went our own ways. All of which, in retrospect, is further proof that the emotional ties had never been strong.' His shoulders moved. 'I'd resigned from the law firm when a friend said he was off to sail around the Caribbean and would I like to join him? With so much to sort out in my head, getting away seemed a great idea.'

Abby frowned. 'And on arrival you sorted out that you wanted to own boats?'

'I was given the opportunity to own boats,' he corrected.

She cast him a glance. Given was his version, but would *taking* the opportunity be nearer the truth? she wondered. His departure from law had been innocent enough, yet her suspicions about his quickfire success in the chartering world refused to disappear.

'Although the divorce had been immaculate it didn't stop me from feeling grubby, and the more I thought about it the more I began to blame myself,' Josh continued. 'I decided that Sarah had had a primal need for a child, a need which I'd denied. Unfortunately, the divorce had left the two sets of parents not talking—more sufferers,' he said wryly, 'so my folks couldn't, or wouldn't, tell me how Sarah was getting along. However, her brother and I had stayed friendly so after a while I dropped him a line. My hope was that she'd find someone new and have kids, but he reported that her only interest now was her work. After several months I asked again, and after that, but her love-life remained stuck at zero. And so, despite her calm dismissal of our marriage, an image grew in my mind of Sarah as a broken woman whom life was passing by. A woman *I'd* broken.' He frowned. 'But then, after five years of berating myself, I returned to Australia.'

'Why did you return?' Abby asked.

'Partly because I was desperate to see the place again, and partly because I'd finally accepted that

I couldn't avoid Sarah—and what I'd done to her—for ever. So I packed my bags and flew home. It was wonderful.'

'You found her with a husband and ten offspring?' she said, as he grinned.

'Just the opposite. I rang and asked if we could meet, and she invited me to lunch at the television company where she still worked.' Josh laughed. 'I went along expecting to eat in the staff canteen, but instead I was shown into a private dining-room. Minutes later, Sarah rushed in, all power-dressing in the dark suit with the padded shoulders. She said how nice it was to see me, but she had an important meeting and, sorry, she could only spare half an hour. It turned out she'd moved up from a secretary ages ago and was now a fully-fledged producer and determined careerist.'

Abby's brow creased. 'What had happened to the desperate need to become a mother?'

'That was dismissed as a youthful whim. She reckoned she would have been far too immature to cope with children—and now she thought kids were overrated anyway—and thanked me for having the good sense to refuse. It was the best news I'd heard in years.'

'So the sob story has a happy ending,' she said, as a smile broke across his face.

'Sweetheart, I didn't fly back to Grenada, I tap-danced.'

For a moment or two they grinned at each other, then Abby looked at her watch. 'It's time I tap-danced off to bed,' she decided, finishing her coffee. 'Any idea when the others are likely to be back?'

'If the place is jumping, they might not wander home until the early hours. You go and I'll wash the mugs,' he said as she stood up. 'After a day spent cooking for eight people and listening to guys spill out their life histories, you must be beat.'

A yawn escaped. 'I am,' she had to agree.

Not much later, Abby was in bed. She heard the creak of the boat, the indolent lap of waves, and then. . .nothing.

'Abby? Abby?' a voice called.

Deep asleep one moment, she shot head-thumpingly awake. What had happened? she wondered, lurching upright in the darkness. Who wanted her? And why? Was the boat on fire? Were they about to sink?

'Who is it? What's wrong?' she demanded feverishly.

'It's me, Rod. I need to talk to you.'

She collapsed back on the pillow. Rod? She groaned. Fancy disturbing her in the middle of the night! Though maybe it was not the middle of the night. Maybe she had only been asleep for a few minutes.

'You can talk to me in the morning!' she whispered crossly.

'But I'm feeling real down.'

Abby put despairing hands over her face. 'Go away!' she ordered, through her fingers.

'Just a word.'

Throwing back the sheet, she crossed to the door and flung it open. A light had been left on at the end of the corridor and its rays illuminated the photographer. His face was drawn. His clothes were crumpled. He drooped.

'I'm sorry you're not feeling too good, but I happen to be feeling tired!' Abby informed him in an angry whisper, but then his dejected look touched her and her tone softened. 'Go back to your cabin,' she entreated. 'Everything will seem better in the morning.'

'But I can't sleep,' Rod whined, sounding like a fractious child.

'You can if you try. Go and try, *please*,' she implored, when he began to protest.

'OK.' Shuffling away, he turned. 'If I don't have any luck I'll come back and see you again,' he said, over his shoulder.

'No!' she hissed, but he stumbled on.

Abby was wondering whether she should follow and spell it out that he must *not* return, when the door opposite opened.

'What's the matter?' Josh asked, peering out. With dark hair dishevelled and his eyes glazed, it was clear that he, too, had been fast asleep. 'Are the others home?' he asked, clutching at the waist of what were plainly hastily pulled on black pyjama trousers.

'No, it was Rod,' she said, and explained. 'I hope he doesn't come back,' she sighed.

'He won't, not after I've finished with him,' Josh muttered.

'Don't,' Abby appealed, as he made to stride off along the corridor. She clutched at his arm. 'He's drunk and unhappy, and if you shout at him you'll only make him feel worse. Anyway, chances are he'll fall asleep.'

'And if he doesn't?' Josh demanded.

'If he reappears I'll read the Riot Act, I promise. Look, Rod is a fare-paying customer, so——'

'I don't care who the hell he is! He has no right to come knocking at your door and disturbing you. Hell, next thing you know the bastard'll be wanting to climb into your bed!'

'He won't. He may have been a bit amorous earlier——'

'Oh, yes?'

'—but now he's just melancholy.'

Josh's fist tightened around the pyjamas. 'You think after seeing you in that outfit he's going to *stay* melancholy?' he enquired.

Abby glanced down. In celebration of her visit to the Caribbean she had splashed out on some luxury lingerie-cum-nightwear, and had gone to bed in a cropped, cut-away black lace top and frilly briefs.

'So I keep my door locked,' she replied.

'And have the guy pounding on it at intervals all through the night?'

Her frown acknowledged the problem. 'Suppose I leave my door wide open and my bed noticeably unoccupied?' she suggested, after a moment. 'Then, when Rod comes along, the message that he's not wanted and I'm not prepared to listen will sock him right between the eyes.'

'Sounds effective, but where will you be while this happens?' Josh asked.

'With you.'

His brows rose. 'In my cabin?'

'If you don't mind. Karl and Klaus could come back at any moment so I can't use theirs, and I've told Rod that—that we're involved. Look, if he is going to return it'll be soon so I shan't disturb you for long,' she said, desperate to stop him rebuking the hapless photographer.

Josh's mouth quirked. 'OK, but before I let you in I need a guarantee that you're not going to pounce on me.'

'You've got it!' she assured him stiffly.

With its single bed, louvred wardrobe and chest of drawers, his cabin was identical to hers. A wall lamp glowed golden, revealing a shelf of paperbacks, a travel poster, discarded plimsolls.

'I'm whacked,' Josh pronounced, and climbed back beneath the sheet. After a minute or two, he raised his head and looked at her. 'Fine, you're not pouncing, but there's no rule which demands you must stand. You are allowed to sit down. I shan't scream.'

Flushing, Abby sat gingerly on the end of the

bed. 'Why don't I switch off the light and let you get some sleep?' she suggested.

'Whatever you wish,' he replied wearily.

The bedside lamp was doused and she returned to her perch. Abby heard the creak of the boat, and the sound of Josh breathing. He was so near. So close. Her back a ramrod, she sat and stared into the blackness, every nerve and fibre janglingly aware of his long body stretched out beside her. She frowned. Coming into his room had been a madcap idea. Why had she ever suggested it? A few minutes ago it had seemed rational, but now. . . She dreaded to think what Freud would have made of her motivation!

'This isn't working. There's no way I can sleep while you're with me, pretending to be a totem pole,' Josh said, all of a sudden. Abby felt the mattress dip and him reaching up, then the light came on. 'Tell me about your boyfriend,' he requested.

She blinked against the glare. 'My boyfriend?'

'The guy who had problems with the gnome—was it a serious relationship?' he asked, sitting up to stuff two pillows behind him. 'Did you live together?'

'Yes. Glynn and I intended to get married.' She glanced at him. 'But as your marriage was a mistake, so ours would have been, too.'

'Why?'

'Because, although we were very fond of each other, there was never much excitement.' Abby made a face. 'Our relationship could be described as comfortable, but drab.'

'How long were you together?'

'Three years.'

'Longer than I was married,' Josh reflected.

'Yes, but for the second two it was mainly force of habit which kept us going. And when we did eventually part, no one wept and no one shouted.'

'You didn't throw things at him?' he enquired.

'No.'

'Have you thrown things at anyone else?'

'Just you.'

Josh reached forward and brushed his knuckles across her thigh. 'You know what that means?' he murmured.

Abby's heart raced. Her skin tightened. He only had to touch her, and longings were triggered off, desires, an instinctive need.

'No,' she lied.

'Yes, you do.' He caught hold of her hand and gently, but determinedly, began to pull her towards him.

'Josh,' she protested, but he gave a final tug which tipped her off balance and, as she fell against him, his mouth covered hers.

The chatterbox in her head told Abby to get up and go, but he began to whisper his desire and caress her—and the chatterbox went ignored. He fondled the roundness of her breasts, and as her nipples hardened beneath the lace she strained against him, the victim of a sweet, sweet ache. It had not been like this with Glynn, she thought dizzily. Never. Ever.

With a satisfied murmur, Josh drew her down with him on to the bed. His kisses became hungrier, his caresses more sensual. He wrapped his arms around her, moulding her to the muscular strength of his body and forcing her to acknowledge the masculine need which she had inspired.

'I want to touch you and kiss you and lick every part of you,' he said, and peeled away the black lace top.

'I thought you liked breasts to be mysterious,' Abby murmured.

Josh drew back, his eyes dark blue and their lids heavy with passion. 'Not yours, sweetheart,' he said huskily.

He held her breasts, savouring their weight and the smoothness of the skin which he told her was like hot velvet. Tracing the outline of her nipple with his finger, he watched it pucker and then bent his head to rasp his tongue roughly around first one taut peak and then the other. Lost in a blur of passion, Abby arched against him.

'As you know, I'm also a fan of the rearward part of your anatomy,' Josh whispered, and eased off her lacy briefs.

When she was naked, he began to stroke her again, rubbing her breasts in circles, then sliding his long fingers down across her hips to dip into the heated centre of her body.

'Josh,' she sighed.

He touched her again and Abby cried out, a

shudder breaking between her legs. Urgently, he stripped away his own clothes, and as his body covered hers she felt the heated thrust of his thighs. That sweet ache built into a driving need, an agony of want, and desperately she clutched at him, her nails digging into his shoulders. His body buried in hers, he moved faster and deeper, until, in a whirling, rampaging, uncontrollable rush of rapture, he possessed her.

CHAPTER SEVEN

IT was a shame-faced and hungover Rod who apologised to Abby the following morning. 'I don't have total recall,' he confessed when he sidled into the galley to speak to her, 'but I know I made a pass at you. Please accept my apology.'

She smiled. 'Apology accepted.'

'Didn't I come along to your cabin and complain about not being able to sleep?'

'That's right.'

'I don't remember anything after that, so——' He rubbed a pensive thumb across the bristles of his moustache. '—I guess I must have zonked out.'

'You never heard the girls?' Abby enquired.

Rod shook his head, then winced against the pain. 'What time did they come back?'

'After three.'

The dance-goers had returned at twenty minutes past, to be precise. Abby knew that because, after succumbing to the languor which followed lovemaking and subsequently falling asleep, she had awoken with a start to find herself lying stiff and numb in the too-small bed. Beside her, taking up most of the room, Josh had slept like a golden-skinned giant. She had tried to settle down again but, now conscious of the restricted space, had not succeeded. With a sigh she had gathered up her clothes and crept back to her own cabin for, much as she would have preferred to stay with him, if she was to function properly the next day it had been important that she get some sleep. Minutes later an outboard had buzzed, waves had slurped, and smothered giggles had announced a belated return. A look at her wristwatch had told her the time.

'I assume the girls are still in bed?' Rod asked.

She nodded. 'And Karl and Klaus.'

'Best place to be. If it's all right with you, I'll have a cup of coffee and a piece of dry toast, then I'll lie down, too.'

'You don't want to go snorkelling, or fishing, or maybe hire a windsurfer?' Josh suggested, coming in. 'It's your last chance.'

The older man looked stricken. 'All I want is a quiet day.'

He had his wish.

Although Josh woke his crewmen mid-morning, it was gone noon before the girls appeared, by which time their breakfast had slid into brunch. The previous evening, so they reported, had been 'wicked', but the heat, the pound of the music, and being constantly on their feet had worn them out and now they were listless.

'It seemed as if every guy in the hall wanted to dance with us,' Sidonie said, half preening and half in complaint.

'Needed to check that what they were seeing

wasn't a bizarre trick of the light,' Josh muttered in an undertone.

Later the anchor was lifted and the *Oz Six* ploughed off through turquoise waves. When they reached the northern tip of Grenada, they stopped for a swim and, because the New York flight checked in mid-evening, an early dinner. Then, with the sun a blazing orange disc sinking slowly in the west, the yacht started on its final stretch for home. Down the leeward coast they sailed, passing towns and villages which Abby had previously visited by car.

'Glad you made the trip?' Josh asked when she joined him in the cockpit.

'It's been inspirational,' she declared.

He placed an arm around her shoulders and brushed his lips against her brow. 'I couldn't have put it better myself,' he murmured.

'Because now I know what to draw for Theo's cartoons,' she finished.

'Nothing else has inspired you?' he enquired, with the outer tilt of a brow.

She undertook a solemn consideration. 'Can't think of anything.'

'Then how about this?' Josh demanded, and his mouth was against hers, his tongue was between her lips, her mouth was opening.

'I'm inspired,' she murmured, a little while later, but his kisses continued. 'I thought business etiquette insisted on discretion?' she asked, when he had finally released her.

'I am being discreet,' he protested. 'What I

really want to do is tear off your clothes and make love to you on deck, but instead I'm restricting myself to a chaste kiss or two.'

Abby's mouth curved. 'Chaste?'

'Everyone else is below getting packed and we're here alone. What else do you expect?'

She smiled into the mesmeric blue of his eyes. 'I expect you to kiss me again. Please.'

It was dark when the *Oz Six* slid into the boat-yard and nudged against the jetty. Ropes were tied, luggage unloaded, then came the moment of departure. The girls shrilled noisy farewells, while Rod mumbled that he wanted Abby to know he would be making a determined effort to control his drinking.

'Peace,' Josh said, as a taxi whisked his clients off to the airport. 'For the next twelve hours.'

'And then you're off on another charter,' she said, recalling what he had told her earlier.

He sighed. 'I wish I didn't have to go.' He reached for her, holding her so tightly against him that she could feel the beat of his heart. 'I wish we could be together. Abby, how am I going to survive fourteen days without you?' he implored.

'You'll manage,' she assured him lightly, though she was wondering the same thing herself.

'When I get back I have a free week and we'll spend every minute of it together. OK?'

'OK,' she smiled.

'We have a lot to talk about, a lot to discuss,' Josh declared, then frowned. He appeared to be toying with the idea of saying something now, something of importance, until a backward glance at Klaus and Karl dissuaded him. 'Keep safe,' he said, and sent her off with a swift kiss.

At the bungalow, Hilda was waiting. She wanted to know which islands Abby had visited, how she had enjoyed life afloat, whether the meals had been a success.

'Everything was fine,' Abby said, reaching the end of a lengthy, happy and discreetly censored report. Maybe tomorrow she would own up to having fallen in love, but this evening it would remain her own private, beautiful secret. 'How about the *Calinargo*?' she enquired casually. 'Has everything been fine there, too?'

'No.'

'No?' she echoed, her eyes widening. 'Why? What's happened?'

The older woman gave a tense smile and sat straighter, and all of a sudden it became clear that her questions had been a stalling, a biding of time, a postponement of the evil moment. 'Josh hasn't told you? How odd. You have been together morning, noon and night.'

Abby felt the stirring of unease. 'Told me what?' she enquired.

'That he's altered his cruises.' Hilda sighed. 'Unfortunately it means that for the last two outings our numbers have been down.'

'By how much?'

'Roughly a third.'

'A third?' she repeated in dismay.

'I'm afraid so. Of course, the business is still making a profit and will still be saleable, but—well, we're not the success story which we were. I suppose it was too good to last. Now we must be realistic and——'

'How has Josh altered his cruises?' Abby demanded.

'For a start, the *Hummingbird*'s been painted and equipped with new seating.'

Her brow furrowed. 'When did that happen? Good grief, I've only been away three days.'

'Apparently the first excursion of the week was cancelled in order for the boat to spend time at Josh's yard. That's where the refurbishment took place.'

'But I was at the yard at the beginning of the week,' she protested.

Hilda gave a rueful nod. 'Seems you must have missed the *Hummingbird* by a whisker. It was returned to the harbour and made the first of its revamped cruises that day.'

Abby thought back. On finding her on his yacht, Josh had not only been startled but had seemed ill at ease—and now she knew why. His tension might have had something to do with the New Yorkers, but it had owed a darn sight more to the thought of her discovering his hush-hush activities!

'What else has Josh done?' she asked, her heart heavy.

'He's had a glass-bottom window installed,' her aunt said, almost apologetically.

'So now his passengers can sit in the dry and look at the underwater life, which ours can't—and won't, because the shape of the *Calinargo* makes it impossible for one to be installed.'

'I don't consider a glass-bottom window to be vital, dear,' Hilda demurred.

'Lots of people like them.' Abby frowned. 'And has the *Hummingbird*'s timetable been changed?'

Her aunt nodded. 'Josh provides barbecue lunches with a choice of either steak or flying fish or chicken. They—um—also serve apple pie and ice-cream for dessert.'

'The louse!' she exclaimed.

'We always knew he'd give as good as he got,' Hilda pointed out hesitantly.

'But he's giving much better!' she retorted, her eyes beginning to blaze. 'Anything else?' she demanded.

Her aunt cleared her throat. 'His passengers are being offered the free use of bumper boats. They're round, motorised inflatables, a sailing version of fairground bumper cars,' she explained. 'Children and young people love them.'

'I bet they do!' Abby said acidly.

'Josh has arranged for the boats to be waiting in the bay when the *Hummingbird* arrives.'

'And he has all the contacts and pull in Grenada's sailing circles.'

'I suppose he does,' the older woman agreed, wondering where this was leading.

'Whereas you and I wouldn't stand a chance of

arranging something similar at anywhere near the same price.'

'But do we want to arrange something?' Hilda asked, plucking at her silver curls. 'We are supposed to be conducting a short-term and budget-wise experiment.'

Abby's mouth pinched. 'You're happy for your future prosperity to be stolen away?' she demanded.

'No, but——' Unable to assemble an argument in the face of such indignation, her aunt gave a tentative smile. 'And Josh didn't mention any of this?'

'He did not give a single hint!' she declared, fiercely nailing down the words.

If Abby had not been fierce, tears would have overtaken her. Josh's retaliation with such a veritable *multitude* of attractions felt like a kick in the teeth, but what hurt most was his silence. It made her feel victimised and double-crossed. Why couldn't he have told her about the *Hummingbird*'s revitalisation? she wondered. Why had he deceived her? As Hilda had said, they had been together for three days, *and* she had been doing him a favour!

Her aunt went to the desk. 'This is his new leaflet,' she said, passing over a glossy fold-out bearing a coloured photograph of a swishly restyled *Hummingbird*. 'Everybody has one. The island's been swamped. They're in all the hotels, all the restaurants, all the shops.'

'Your cruise will be enhanced by the courteous

and personal attention of our crew,' Abby read, her eyes skimming down. 'Josh has replaced Leroy?'

'A man who used to skipper his yachts has agreed to come out of retirement and be captain,' Hilda told her. 'I know him through my bridge games. He's a real gentleman.'

Abby glowered. 'Something which Josh Donner is not!'

Minutes after the new-look *Hummingbird* had sailed out of the boat-yard, she must have walked in—yet those sculpted lips had been remained firmly buttoned, he had not uttered a squeak. She had, Abby was forced to admit, kept quiet about the *Calinargo* lunches, but that was different. Josh had not been in proximity at the time and they had not been friends, let alone lovers. Lovers! Her stomach knotted. When she had met Glynn she had been a virgin, and they had not slept together until a secure relationship had been established. But what was secure about her relationship with Josh—nothing! He had forced her to acknowledge that she loved him, but was the feeling reciprocated or could sleeping with her have been a straightforward exercise in sexual gratification? A shaky hand was pushed through her hair. Had she been double-crossed in love as well as in business? She frowned. How it had happened she did not know, but somehow she had lost sight of how she did not trust him. Love was ever blind, Abby thought miserably. She had decided he was Mr Nice Guy, but, as everyone knew, nice guys don't win ball games.

Her thoughts returned to the *Calinargo*. Having reduced their trade—which must reduce the chances of selling the schooner—did Josh now intend to stroll back with his 'as is' offer and, being in the right place at the right time, grab himself a bargain? Abby's mouth compressed. Her shoulders straightened. The only way he would grab himself a bargain would be over her dead body!

'Bumper boats,' she read, focusing on the leaflet again. 'Right, *we'll* have an extra attraction.'

'Do you think we should?' Hilda said doubtfully.

'Why not? We've recouped our start-up expenses and made some money besides, so we can afford it.'

'Well, yes, though——'

Abby's eyes glittered. 'Your future is at stake here, and I intend to safeguard it,' she announced importantly.

'Thank you,' her aunt said, 'but——'

'So we must regain the offensive. How about hiring a calypso group?' Abby steamrollered on. 'They could play Caribbean melodies on the way out and provide music for dancing on the sail back. Then we can advertise our cruises as "party" cruises,' she said, her enthusiasm for the idea growing. 'The *only* party cruise in Grenada, because the *Hummingbird*'s deck space is so limited there's no chance of Josh doing the same!'

Hilda gave a reluctant smile. 'If that's what you feel you must do, dear.'

Although finding someone to produce the appropriate rubber stamp tapped reserves of resourcefulness and patience Abby never realised she possessed, the *Calinargo*'s advertisements soon carried an amendment and the calypso band was on board. Then she walked on pins. Would music and dancing appeal? A couple of outings later the answer was provided when the numbers began to climb, but they fell short of the previous totals and another week on remained infuriatingly static.

'As the six-week trial's almost through, shouldn't we put the business up for sale?' Hilda suggested as they drove home one afternoon.

Abby frowned. 'I suppose so, though our current takings aren't going to make anyone a millionaire.'

'Maybe they're not quite as high as they were before, but they're not that bad,' her aunt protested. 'Besides, it's not everyone who wants to be a millionaire.'

'I think we should advertise, but do our best to drum up more customers in the meantime,' she declared, her hands tightening around the steering-wheel.

'You wouldn't be—er—willing to settle for the status quo?'

'No! We have the rest of your life hanging in the balance,' Abby stated, in a grave reminder.

'I suppose so,' Hilda acknowledged uncertainly.

'I was rereading the brochures of the cruises you and Bob took, and one of them features a boat which is similar to the *Calinargo*. A big thing's made of the pirate angle, so why don't we have Eldon dress as Captain Hook, install a plank for swimmers to walk, and a rope for swinging? It wouldn't cost much and it dovetails beautifully with our advertisement. I think we should also reconsider T-shirts,' she went on. 'I know you said——'

'No T-shirts, not for now,' her aunt rejected hastily. 'Let's just stick with the pirate idea.'

If acquiring the rubber stamp had been fraught with problems, the seemingly simple fitment of a plank and a rope now turned out to be a lesson in one hundred per cent frustration. A day was spent driving around the island and speaking to carpenters, timber merchants and a variety of handymen, but although Abby insisted on seeking out every one listed in the telephone book, all their enquiry received was blank looks and shaken heads.

'The general feeling is that a boat-builder would be our best bet, then when we visit them they won't listen,' she complained at breakfast the next morning. 'You wouldn't like to ring around your friends and see if they have any suggestions?'

Hilda made several calls, and finally managed to rout out a couple of places where vessels had been seen under construction.

'They're both small fishing boats which are being built on a casual basis, but it's possible someone there might be willing to help us. Mind you, it's a long shot,' she warned.

'But worth a try!' Abby declared, determined not to be defeated.

'One boat is at Grand Anse beach and the other's in the north of the island,' her aunt said, and explained the exact locations.

Abby frowned. 'Would you mind if I skipped the *Calinargo* and went to see these people today?'

'Please do—though I suspect you're on a wild-goose chase.'

After delivering Hilda to the harbour, Abby drove the few miles to her first stop: the beach. Parking the car in the shade of a spreading banyan tree, she walked down to the sand. In the far distance, and partly obscured by palms, she spotted the skeleton of a boat, so she shed her sandals, put on her sunglasses, and set off towards it.

There were two magical things about Grand Anse, Abby reflected as she strolled by the edge of the sea. One was the beauty of the two-mile stretch of white coral sand, and the other was that you could walk along it without being required to step over bodies or swerve to avoid ball games. At the other end of the bay a smattering of guests at the beachfront hotels lay sunbathing, but the only people in her vicinity were a couple cycling the ocean on a big-wheeled pedalo.

She walked on. The boat came into focus. Abby was swerving up towards it when her stride abruptly faltered. Beyond the palms she saw no workmen, no activity, no sign of life. Work on the vessel must have ceased a while ago, for when she got closer she discovered that the wood was weathered and sun-bleached. Hissing out a sigh, she turned. It had been a wasted journey. Another one. Or had it? she thought, gazing at the tempting blue of the sea. Her bikini and towel were in the car and half an hour's swim would leave plenty of time to drive north.

The towel hooked around her, Abby stood in the shelter of the car door and stripped off her clothes, but when she reached in for her bikini it had gone. Made from a silky white material, both bra-top and skimpy bottom had slithered down between the front seats and on to the floor. With a sigh she stretched to retrieve them, and was half-in and half-out of the Ford when an engine roared. The next moment, a vehicle bumped down the track which led from the road and swung in alongside. Why did the driver need to park so close, Abby wondered, and at such an inconvenient time? Unsettled at being caught undressed, she grabbed at the elusive scraps of silk. Hastily, she stepped into the bikini pants, tripping over her feet and almost falling. She had yanked them up and was engaged in some frantic under-towel contortions aimed at locating the straps of the top, when a masculine laugh sounded behind her.

'Congratulations, you're retaining all the mystery,' an Australian voice drawled.

Abby's head jerked up. She spun round. All movement beneath the towel ceased. 'Why is it you always appear when I'm least expecting you?' she enquired, her eyes the grey of freezing water.

Josh climbed out of the Moke and slammed the door. 'You bloody well *should* be expecting me!' he retorted. 'The last time we were together, you were asking to be kissed—remember?'

She hauled the towel closer around her. 'Yes,' she muttered.

'And do you also remember that my charter finished last night?' he demanded. She nodded. 'So what happened?'

'The *Hummingbird happened*,' Abby said fiercely. 'The painting, the seating, the glass-bottom window, the multi-choice barbecue lunches, *ad infinitum*. You said we had a lot to discuss, but it's noticeable that you never bothered to say a single word about any of them!'

Josh's jaw tightened. 'I was going to, but——'

'Like hell you were! I arrive at your boat-yard and miss the *Hummingbird*'s face-lift by what appear to have been seconds, yet what do you say? Zilch. Then, when you've got me out of the way, the grand relaunch takes place. Sorry, but I don't appreciate a myriad attractions appearing behind my back!'

'You reckon I orchestrated it that way? What kind of a guy do you think I am?' he protested. 'For a start, it was Theo who suggested you act as cook, not me, so he's the one who was responsible for your absence. But even if I'd wanted to stage-manage the transformation so that it came together at some special time, do you think I could?' Josh demanded. 'You must've been in Grenada long enough to know that things move at their own speed here, that there can be all kinds of hold-ups. OK, sometimes things happen quickly, but in the main they proceed at snail's pace. And whichever it is you don't have much control. Yes, renovations had been planned—and you knew as much, and accepted it,' he thrust, 'but the fact that the improved *Hummingbird* made its debut when you were gone was pure——'

'Happenstance?' Abby said scornfully, though even as she spoke she accepted that it had been that way.

'Yes.' His affirmative was low and succinct. 'But what about the *Calinargo*'s ballroom orchestra?' he carried on. 'Didn't that make its debut while *my* back was turned and didn't you say damn-all?'

Her chin lifted. 'You weren't with me every day. You were away.'

'But not out of touch,' Josh rapped, his eyes a steely blue, 'or I wouldn't have been if you'd answered my calls. I thought it was odd that on each of the half a dozen occasions when I managed to get to a phone you were out, but yesterday, when Mrs Sinclair told me you were unavailable yet again, I became distinctly suspicious and—for want of a better description—fed-up!' A nerve throbbed in his temple. 'Which is why this morning I decided to bypass the telephone and see you in person. I missed you at the bungalow, so I went along to the harbour and——'

'Hilda told you I'd be here?' Abby cut in, heartily wishing her aunt had kept quiet.

'She did. She also couldn't wait to tell me how you were fixing up for the *Calinargo* to become a *Jolly Roger extraordinaire.*' He bowed a sarcastic head. 'Thanks a bunch. May I applaud the Empire for striking back—yet again!'

'You expect us not to?' Abby protested. The aim was to be dignified and aloof, but as she was currently squirming to fasten the bikini top she had scant success.

'I don't expect you to be so damn greedy,' Josh rasped.

'We're not!' she said, and, bikini at last in place, flung the towel into the car.

A second later, she regretted the action for, with long fingers spread on his hips and his gaze insolent, Josh began a leisurely appraisal of her body. The bikini was small, but beneath his eyes it shrank to alarmingly wanton proportions. Abby felt her cheeks burn. He seemed to be deliberately reminding her of how she had lain naked with him and given herself up in abandoned surrender.

'We're not being greedy,' she said again, desperate to shatter the moment and end his inspection.

He bestirred himself. 'Let's not sugar-coat the facts,' he rasped. 'It's clear that your one aim is to grab every last customer and to hell with my business.' He gave a strangled laugh. 'I had some crazy notion you cared for me, but all you care about is going one better, one better, one bloody better!'

Abby frowned, shaking her had. 'No.'

'Irresistible force intends to polish off immovable object,' Josh defined caustically.

'I don't want to polish off the *Hummingbird*,' she muttered.

'Then what the hell do you want?' he demanded.

She started to speak, then faltered. She had been about to say that, for her aunt's sake, she wanted to boost the *Calinargo*'s trade and thus the selling price, but, in truth, the number of passengers she had been attempting to claw back would not greatly affect the amount they hoped to obtain from the eventual sale. Would probably not affect it at all. Abby frowned. She had claimed to be helping Hilda, but wasn't that simply an excuse for no-holds-barred revenge? And when she had talked about regaining the offensive, hadn't her aim been to inflict damage on Josh *per se*?

'You have your bumper boats,' she said, in a defensive swerve.

'All they were supposed to do was even things up, which they did until you introduced party-time,' he said coldly.

'Even things up?' she repeated, the novelty of the idea sending her voice soaring several octaves.

'Yes! To me, the *Hummingbird* and the *Calinargo* sailing with near enough the same number of passengers seemed reasonable. *Very* reasonable, when you recall that I operate three cruises per week, while you have the lion's share of four!'

Her frown deepened, and suddenly everything took on a different perspective. It had not been Josh who had gone over the top with his attractions, she realised in dismay—it was her. Pangs of remorse hit. Bringing in the calypso group had been a knee-jerk reaction, Abby thought uneasily. A wild hitting back. She had never stopped to consider the equality of their trade, nor that Josh might merely have been attempting to draw level. On starting up the cruises the question of fair play had worried her, but latterly she had not given it a moment's thought.

A strand of hair was twisted unhappily around her finger. 'I seem to have——' she started.

'Please let me finish,' he bit out. 'And reasonable when you also consider the *Hummingbird*'s passenger capacity is limited so that any growth in business will automatically fall your way.'

Abby's heart sank. What he said was true *and* reasonable. It also made a nonsense of the theory that his ambition was to wreck their trade and grab the *Calinargo* at a knock-down price. Yes, Josh had been secretive, but so had she. And he had not attempted to murder her with a chainsaw—all he had done was come back with some perfectly admissible competition. Her mistrust ground to a shuddering halt. Suddenly, she felt deeply ashamed. She had rushed into certain presumptions which had led her to decide that he was an opportunist, though now she did not know why. Regrets flooded in. Abby wished everything between them had not happened so quickly. She wished she knew him better. She wished she had had the sense to ask him to explain his business success.

'Josh——' she began afresh, but his anger now had a determined momentum.

'Although your dance band destroyed the balance again, there was a chance I'd have accepted it,' he went on, 'but not now. Not since I heard about your pirate tricks. You started all this,' he said, jabbing an accusing finger, 'but, make no mistake, *I* shall finish it. Maybe Bob Sinclair did leave a rich widow who's happy to finance these little games of yours, but——'

Abby stared. 'Who said my aunt was rich?' she demanded.

'You did. When I asked if she was short of money, you made it clear she had plenty.'

Her toes curled into the sand. The haywire situation made it imperative that Josh be told the truth, but it was Hilda's truth, and a rigorously protected one, so before anything was said shouldn't she be consulted?

'Oh, oh, yes,' Abby mumbled.

'As I was saying,' Josh continued, 'maybe Mrs Sinclair is well off, but it's time she considered where this is going to end.'

'What do you mean?' she enquired, alert to the granite edge of a threat in his voice.

'Suppose the bumper boats are joined by jet

skis and windsurfers and parasailing? Is she prepared to lay out more and more cash to equip the *Calinargo* with more and more attractions? Think about it,' he instructed.

Abby *was* thinking. Her head had never been so busy, and now it throbbed with a new batch of complications. She put a worried hand to her brow. 'But if you bring in jet skis and—and everything, our trade will plummet and we may never be able to sell the schooner,' she faltered.

Josh arched a brow. 'You still want to sell? You and your aunt aren't having such a ball you've decided not to bother?'

Her toes curled deeper. 'Of course we're bothering.'

'Then let's hope the next owners are a lot less bloody-minded than you!' he said savagely. 'I've heard about ambition, but it wasn't until recently I realised Attila the Hun was alive and well and operating a schooner in Grenada!' Josh pushed his hands into his pockets and regarded her in silence for an appreciable length of time. 'And to think,' he said eventually, 'I once thought you and I were——'

'We were what?' Abby asked, when he broke off.

'It doesn't matter.' Narrowing his eyes, he looked beyond her at the sea. 'She's a fine craft,' he muttered.

As she turned to follow his gaze, Abby saw that the *Calinargo* was sailing past. Her sails plump with breeze and brightly coloured flags fluttering, the schooner cut cleanly through the waves. With twin masts standing tall and proud, she was an elegant reminder of bygone days.

'But the *Hummingbird*'s looking pretty swanky, too,' she protested.

Icy blue eyes met hers. 'A swanky hamburger carton,' Josh said, and swung into the Moke.

Abby took an urgent step forward. Her escalation of the *Calinargo*'s attractions would end, right now. She would not drive north. She would not locate a plank and a rope. The pirate idea would be scrapped. It *must* be, if she was to have any peace of mind, if she was ever to be able to live with herself again. She would withdraw the calypso band, too.

'About the *Calinargo*——' she began.

'Forget it,' Josh ordered. 'I've had the damn thing, and you, up to——' a hand was levelled beneath his chin '—here.'

'But——'

'Goodbye,' he said, and drove away.

A swim had lost its appeal. Abby changed back into her clothes, then sat for a long time in the car. Their relationship had been full of promise and could have been so *good*, but by her foolish distrust she had wrecked it, she thought despairingly. All she felt towards him now was love, and all he felt for her was hostility. She brushed away hot tears. She did not want Josh to be hostile, she wanted—— Thrusting the key into the ignition, she gunned the engine. What did it matter? He had made his feelings perfectly plain.

When Abby returned to the bungalow, she reached instinctively for her sketch pad. Drawing always took her mind off things, and there was nothing to be gained from mooching dejectedly around thinking about Josh and what might have been. In any case, she was in the midst of preparing Theo's sketches and cartoons and this seemed the ideal opportunity to finish them. Sitting down at the desk, she filled one page, and then another, and another. She broke off at lunchtime to make a sandwich, but when she next looked at the clock she stared in disbelief. The arrangement had been for her to collect Hilda when the cruise ended, but that was thirty minutes ago.

Castigating herself for her tardiness, she drove down to the harbour. Her aunt had said she would wait if there was a delay, and as Abby swung the Ford on to the quay she saw her patiently standing there.

'I'm so sorry,' she gabbled, leaping out of the car, 'but I was drawing and time slipped by and—and I never meant to be late.'

'I'm glad you were.'

'Why?' she asked suspiciously, for it had registered that the older woman was beaming and looking supremely self-satisfied.

'Because while I was waiting here someone arrived and asked if I'd sell them the *Calinargo*. And I did.'

'You've sold it?' Abby said, her eyes wide and incredulous. 'To whom?'

'Josh.'

Her nerves shrieked. Her stomach twisted. She had been so convinced of his integrity, but now. . . Pictures of how he had admired the *Calinargo* and derided the *Hummingbird* flicked through her head, closely followed by the knowledge that Hilda had always been enamoured and how, when faced with his threat of jet skis and such, would easily be persuaded. So Josh had worked his blue-eyed magic and finally achieved his 'as is' price! Abby felt wretched, wounded, cut. His faults might not be visible to the naked eye, but, she thought as her heart bled, he fitted the description of original flawed hero: good-looking, intelligent, tender—and as crafty as hell!

'Why did you let him have it?' she wailed. 'If we'd advertised the boat as a business, someone else would have wanted it and offered more. Much more.'

'I doubt it.'

'How much did he give you?' she demanded.

'The same price that Bob was offered,' Hilda said serenely.

Abby gaped. 'You mean——?'

'I mean,' her aunt said with a smile, 'Josh has made sure I shall live comfortably for ever after.'

CHAPTER EIGHT

ABBY worked her way around her suitcase flicking down safety catches, then turned the key in the lock.

'Almost ready,' she announced as she walked into the living-room. Guilt began to nibble. 'You're sure you'll be all right on your own?'

'Positive.' Hilda smiled, which was just as well because, guilty or not, Abby had no intention of changing her plans. 'I have some good friends here and, besides, your mother's promised to join me for Christmas and that's not far away. Then in the spring I'll be returning to England.' She sighed. 'It's just a pity you're leaving at such short notice. I know you've been here far longer than either of us ever expected, dear, but yesterday I sell the *Calinargo* and today you're gone. It's so sudden.'

'The UK flights are fully booked, and according to the airline if I don't take up tonight's cancellation there might not be another seat available for ages,' she explained for about the third time. 'And I need to get back to work.'

Her aunt nodded. 'I understand.'

No, you don't, Abby said silently. Work came a poor second; the top priority was removing herself from Grenada—and Josh.

Her gaze went to the desk and the large brown envelope which sat there. All afternoon it had been waiting to be delivered, and all afternoon she had found reasons to delay. The envelope could, of course, always be sent by post, but that would be cowardly—and good manners dictated that, given the chance, she must thank her aunt's benefactor for his munificence. Abby made a face. The irony was that Hilda's security had rated as a by-product. The reason Josh had bought the schooner was because he had been sick to death of the hassle it involved, and of *her*.

She lifted the envelope. 'I'll go and see if Theo's at the boat-yard and give him my drawings,' she said. 'I won't be long.'

'Don't forget to say goodbye to Josh,' Hilda instructed.

Her smile was tight. 'I won't.'

Although Abby hoped—gave up fervent appeals to the gods—he would not be around, the real ordeal, she acknowledged as she drove along, would be forgetting about *him*. Right now her erstwhile lover occupied her every thought, and although by tomorrow she would have placed thousands of miles between them she had an unhappy feeling that distance was not going to make much difference.

When she opened the office door, she saw the coloured girl busy at her typewriter.

'Hello.' Abby smiled.

The fingers stopped tapping. 'Hi.'

'Good afternoon,' a familiarly deeper voice said

as she stepped inside, and she found Josh checking dates on a wall planner.

Although she had promised herself that when they met again—if they met—she would be the ultimate in cool poise, it did not happen. Instead her heart began to beat like a tom-tom, her throat went dry, she knew that she blushed scarlet.

'Oh—oh, hello,' Abby replied chokily, cursing herself for such a pathetic reaction.

'You've saved me a journey. I was on my way to see you,' Josh explained, when she frowned. 'I've been on my way all day, but this morning formalising the purchase of the *Calinargo* took longer than expected. However, the money's now been transferred to Mrs Sinclair's account. And this afternoon——' he made a regretful grimace '—I've been consistently side-tracked.'

Abby flashed a smile. 'Thanks for letting me know about the money; I'll tell my aunt. And—and thank you for buying the *Calinargo*. It means a lot to me.' She turned to the girl. 'I've brought some sketches for Theo.'

'I'm sorry, but he's away.'

'In that case I'd like to leave this,' she said, and handed over the envelope. 'There's an explanatory letter inside.'

'Theo'll be back in a couple of days,' Josh told her, 'so why not hang on to the sketches and speak to him then? I know he's eager to speak to you. Apparently——'

'I won't be here,' Abby cut in. 'I'm leaving in a few hours.' She stuck out a formal hand. 'I'd like to say goodbye. I realise I went too far with the *Calinargo*, and—and I apologise.'

'You're flying out tonight?' he protested, showing complete disregard for her proffered fingers. 'But you can't!'

Her brow crinkled. 'Why not?'

'Because——' Josh began, then stopped short, aware of his secretary's pricked ears. 'Come with me and I'll tell you,' he said and, catching hold of Abby's wrist, he drew her through the door, out of the cabin and into the sunshine. A flagged path cut between the green lawns and, at full tilt, he began propelling her along it.

'Hold on,' Abby protested. In readiness for the plane journey she had caught her freshly washed hair into a *soignée* twist and had changed into scarlet trousers and a light matching coat, with a white top beneath. On her feet were high-heeled sandals. But now, thanks to the pace he set, her hair was tumbling loose, the flounced coat swirled and she was having to half jog, half totter in the spindly heels. 'Where are you taking me?' she gasped, as he dragged her in his wake.

'To my house. We need to talk, in private.'

She stopped in her tracks. 'There isn't time,' she protested. 'I have a plane to catch.'

'There's plenty of time,' Josh rasped, and pulled her forward again, skipping and skittering, until they reached the car park. Here he released her and opened the passenger door of his Moke. 'Get in,' he instructed.

Abby stood firm. 'I'm sorry, but——'

'Get *in*!' he thundered, his glare making it plain that anything less than instant obedience would result in her being yanked off her feet and thrown bodily inside. 'Why are you leaving so quickly?' Josh demanded, as Abby did as she was told and the Moke roared into life.

'Why would I stay?' she countered. 'My aunt's affairs are in order now, and—and I need to get back to work.'

The fact that she was also leaving because he had had enough of her was left unsaid. Pride kept her from telling him *that*.

'The reason Theo wants to speak to you is because he's anxious to set up a meeting between you and his publishers,' he said, as he drove up the ramp. 'He's shown them your West Indian drawings and it seems they're keen for you to illustrate a guidebook.' Josh frowned at a gardener who, having noticed his boss's flight with an argumentative blonde, was resting on his hoe to watch. 'Plus a firm who publish postcards and prints have a couple of propositions. So, if you decided to stay in Grenada you could continue with your career.'

'Maybe. However, there's not much point because my aunt will also be departing in a few months' time.' As Abby began to reassemble what had been revealed as an overly ambitious hairstyle, she frowned. Although she would soon be gone, she did not want him to think *too* badly of her. 'About Hilda's affairs; Bob Sinclair didn't leave a rich widow, he left a—a poor one,' she said, beginning a jerky explanation.

'I know.'

She shot him a startled glance. 'Hilda told you?'

'No, though her relief when I said I wanted to buy the *Calinargo* made it patently clear. You told me. Not in so many words,' he said, when she stared at him, 'but yesterday when I talked about arranging the jet skis, you looked so distraught that you started me thinking. OK, it's impossible to be cast-iron certain of anyone else's finances, yet Bob Sinclair appeared to be moderately affluent and nothing more. I thought about that, and the stories I'd heard of how he and his wife had been living it up for a year, and suddenly everything was so obvious. I understood why you'd grabbed at my mention of cruises as if it were a life-saver and why you'd been dedicated to coming out on top. You weren't playing games,' he said soberly, 'you were acting out of necessity.'

Abby frowned. 'The cruises were started in the hope of helping Hilda, but later, when I brought in the calypso group, my motives weren't so noble.' She skewered in the final silver pin. 'I didn't like being kept in the dark about the *Hummingbird* and—well, I decided you were out to annihilate our trade and snatch the *Calinargo*. I wanted to tell you the truth about Hilda's finances,' she said, shying away from describing the doubts which now translated as insults, 'but she's keen that no one knows how rash Bob was.'

'And no one will. I won't say anything,' Josh promised.

'Thank you,' she said gratefully.

As they rounded a bend, his house appeared on the hill. He drove up the red-paved drive, and parked the Moke beneath the shade of the pillared portico.

'Out!' he instructed, when she hesitated and frowned at her watch.

Abby got out. 'Thank you again for buying the *Calinargo*,' she said as he ushered her indoors. 'I thought you'd bought it because you were fed up wasting so much time and having so much trouble, but now I see you were also rescuing my aunt.'

'Wrong!' Josh declared. 'I bought it to rescue *us*.'

Abby's heart leapt. 'Us?' she queried cautiously.

He lead her to the sofa, where he sat down beside her. 'The *Calinargo*, and the cruises, have been fouling things up ever since we met,' Josh said earnestly. 'You know why I kept quiet about the alterations to the *Hummingbird*? Because I was certain that if I told you we'd end up quarrelling. Theo accused me of shoddy practice when you came to the boat-yard and I kept quiet, and I guess he was right. But although I was tempted to tell you I chickened out, and hoped instead that when you found out for yourself you'd understand. Later, when we were on the *Oz Six*, I intended to say something, but I never seemed able to get round to it and, hell, Abby,' he complained, 'every time the cruises were mentioned they spoiled things between us.'

She looked at him. 'Like the night I came to dinner?'

'Just like that,' he said heavily, and sighed. 'After we made love I was this close to telling you——' his thumb and forefinger indicated a millimetre '—yet still I held back. I couldn't bear to risk souring our relationship. It was very new, and the attraction between us had been so sudden and. . .overwhelming.' He gave a twisted grin. 'I needed to keep that special feeling which we'd created alive, and it *was* special,' he insisted. 'I may have tap-danced back from Australia, but I didn't sail home to Grenada with you two weeks ago—I floated on a pink cloud.'

'And me.' Abby smiled.

'Yet you still believed I was the kind of ruthless bastard who could make love and try to ruin your cruises at the same time? Why?' he demanded.

She released a breath. 'I think the root cause of it all was how we started off.'

'What do you mean?'

'I'd taken it for granted you were going to buy the *Calinargo* and when you said you weren't I was so thrown and so disappointed that it seemed like a dirty trick. I decided you'd become too successful too quickly to be straight, and so you went from Good Samaritan to con man in two seconds flat.' Abby made a wry face. 'Though in retrospect I can see no proper reason for jumping to such a conclusion.'

Josh pursed his lips. 'I think I can,' he said slowly. 'Bereavement comes at the top of the stress scale, and last year you lose your father and this year you arrive in Grenada to be faced with Robert Sinclair's death. Once again you're put through the wringer, and once again you start living on your emotions.'

'And my reaction was entirely emotional?' she mused. 'You could be right.'

'That's what happened,' he said, in firm assurance.

Abby looked at him and smiled. 'You're making me feel a lot better.'

'Throwing the pencils was also emotional,' he continued, his blue eyes glinting.

'Can't you forget about that?' she implored.

'Sweetheart, no one's ever hurled things at me before.'

She wrinkled her nose. 'Anyway, having more or less decided you were an exponent of dirty tricks, I proceeded to gather what seemed like more evidence.'

'Such as?' Josh enquired.

'I was suspicious of the way you looked at me when we first met. It seemed too. . .discerning. And I didn't trust how you'd turned your nose up at the *Calinargo* and then put in an offer,' she told him. 'Though now I can see that you decided you might as well take it, partly because it was available and partly to do Hilda a favour.'

Josh nodded. 'That's right.'

'But at the time I marked it up against you,'

she said regretfully. 'A few days later, you upped your offer——'

'And chose just the wrong moment,' he put in drily.

'Yes. So although you were helpful and kind, at the back of my mind was the nagging thought that I shouldn't trust you. I do now,' she hurried to tell him. 'I know you're the genuine article.'

He grinned. 'Thanks for the endorsement. But you're not the first person to wonder how I made it from ex-lawyer to boat-yard owner in what, from the outside, appears to have been one easy step.' Josh frowned. 'When I said I was in the right place at the right time, I meant it. I arrived in Grenada a few months after the American troops had landed, and——'

'I know,' Abby cut in. 'Theo told me. He also told me how you met up with a Mr Sissons.'

'Ed,' Josh said, and smiled affectionately. 'Ed Sissons had come here from Toronto a couple of years earlier, full of dreams of running a boating business in the sunshine. Grenada's political troubles had already been simmering but, in his wisdom, he'd decided they'd never amount to anything and had gone ahead with the boat-yard—plus he'd placed orders for six luxury yachts, which were to be delivered at intervals over the next four years.'

'Oh, dear.'

'Ed was not the most astute of forecasters,' Josh said ruefully, 'nor did he ever do anything by halves. When my mate and I appeared enquiring for a sail, we found him sunk in despair because although the fighting was soon over it had effectively killed off the tourist trade. We were the first customers he'd seen in ages, and he was convinced that both Grenada and his dreams were doomed. When we started talking, and the poor guy was desperate to talk, it turned out that he'd spent some of his youth in Australia—which made us bosom pals. He said he had a newly built bungalow and he'd like the company, so would we care to join him and kip down for free?'

Abby grinned, looking around her. 'Here?'

'That's right. Every day my mate and I would sail and later we'd join up with Ed, and every day he'd unburden himself more and more. He'd sent his wife home and now he was obsessed with getting back to Toronto, too, yet although he didn't need the cash he couldn't bring himself to close up the boat-yard and walk away. He reckoned it would be an admission of failure. But neither was he prepared to shut up shop and come back later—which I reckon he should have done.'

'So you made him an offer?'

'No way. I didn't want the boat-yard!' Josh protested.

Abby arched a brow. 'As you didn't want the *Calinargo*?'

'Exactly,' he agreed, his voice dry. 'However, one day Ed declared that my mate and I would make the perfect buyers. Both of us sailed and loved the sea, and whereas he couldn't imagine

Grenada's tourists returning in time to help him, we were both young and the boat-yard would be a good, if long-term, investment. We said thanks, but no, thanks, and explained that in addition to not having anywhere near enough money, my mate was committed to the job he had back home.'

'And then?' she said, when his mouth curved.

'The next day, Ed offered a fresh scenario. I was to be the sole owner, and he'd be happy to do a deal where all I gave him was a fixed percentage of my profit each year—no matter how small an amount that was—until I'd paid for the yard, the house, and the yachts he was committed to take.'

'It must have been a hefty amount,' Abby protested.

'As nobody was buying anything on Grenada at that time, the yard and house came dirt cheap,' Josh explained. 'However, the yachts were pricey.'

'But you agreed?'

He shook his head. 'I'd gone into law and my marriage because it had been expected of me, so the last thing I intended to do was rush into a boating business simply to suit Ed. In any case, although my view of Grenada's tourist revival was a damn sight more optimistic than his, taking on a chartering company under the prevailing circumstances seemed the ultimate in neck-sticking-out exercises. However, Ed refused to drop the idea. He insisted that my arriving without a job, in search of a new career and just released from personal ties, was a coincidence that I couldn't, and shouldn't, ignore. So, to cut the story short, eventually I signed on the dotted line.' Josh made a face. 'I guess having a reason to stay away from Australia, that is, Sarah, played a part, too. I had my share of the proceeds from the sale of the house we'd lived in—and in the two years we were married it had shot up in value—so there was sufficient to make a reasonable down payment to Ed and start me off.'

Abby frowned. 'You couldn't have had many customers yourself to begin with?'

'They were few and far between,' he agreed. 'On one level the deal was extremely advantageous, but it meant I spent the first two years living from hand to mouth. There were many occasions when I sat alone at night biting my nails and wondering what on earth I'd agreed to.'

'And for two years you paid very little to Mr Sissons?'

'Virtually nothing.'

'He didn't mind?'

'Ed was amazingly casual about money, probably because he'd inherited a chunk from his father and had never *needed* to make his own way in the world,' he said whimsically. 'However,' Josh went on, 'in due course a director of a French trucking company chartered one of my yachts. He didn't give a toss about the invasion, which was past history anyhow; what bothered him was good food, good wine and some fantastic sailing—all of which I was able to provide. He went back home and told his friends, and they told their friends, and not much later my charters began to be fully booked.'

'The big time.' She grinned.

'It had its price. I work hard now, but then!'

'Eighteen hours a day?' Abby asked, when he grimaced.

'At least. Apart from the crews, I couldn't afford much in the way of back-up, so I used to handle the bookings, clean the yachts, cut the grass—whatever—myself. Some weeks it seemed as if I never slept. However, at least I was able to start paying off my debts. For two or three years I sent decent sums of money to Ed, but eighteen months ago he died.' Pain flickered in his eyes. 'He left an instruction in his will that I was to be released from any further payments. He didn't have any kids, his wife was well catered for, so—I benefited.'

'He must have been very fond of you,' she said.

'I was fond of him. He used to fly down to Grenada to see me, and we always had a great time,' Josh replied, and brooded for a moment. 'As business continued to flourish I got myself a back-up team, and bought four more yachts—on hire purchase.' He hesitated. 'With regard to my discerning look, I realise this sounds weird but when Mrs Sinclair introduced us I suddenly knew that, whether it was for good or for bad, you were going to have an influence on my life.'

Abby looked at him. 'Sixth sense?' she asked.

'The same.'

'You must have decided it was for bad when I started up the *Calinargo* cruises,' she said ruefully.

'Sweetheart, although I admit I was doing a half-assed job with the *Hummingbird*, when I discovered you'd changed the format and were providing meals—well, if you'd been a bloke I'd have knocked your teeth down your throat. As it was, I hardly complained—which proves something,' Josh mused.

'What?'

'That I must already have been halfway in love with you.'

She smiled. 'And now?'

'You want me to spell it out?' he asked.

Abby hugged the moment around her. 'Every word,' she declared.

He took hold of her hands. 'I love you, *all* the way,' he said seriously.

'And I love you, too.'

'Then you mustn't leave tonight,' Josh insisted, his voice low and ragged. 'Abby, you can't! Stay here with me. *Please*.'

'I suppose I could,' she murmured, as he began kissing her with fevered, coaxing kisses.

'Then that's settled,' he said, full of masculine satisfaction and, with his kisses continuing, he began to slide out the silver pins. 'I like you with your hair down,' he smiled as the blonde skeins fell heavily around her shoulders. He wrapped strands around his hands, capturing her and drawing her closer. 'I also like you without so many damn clothes.'

Her coat and blouse and other garments were dispensed with, and, presently, his shirt. There was much kissing, touching, caressing.

'This is all getting too much for me,' Josh muttered, some time later. 'We shall have to go to bed.'

Pressing his lips to the high globes of her breasts, he began to slowly and tantalisingly kiss his way down her body. His mouth was hot, branding her skin with fervent dedications of his love. His kisses travelled along her torso, and across the curves of her thighs to seek out the secret parts of her. Abby's senses reeled. Her breathing quickened. Waves of longing crashed over her.

'Josh,' she sighed.

His mouth returned to hers and he moved, imprisoning her beneath his body. 'I want you. I've wanted you all my life,' he vowed hoarsely.

The world faded. Only the two of them existed. Skin slid against moisture-sheened skin. Abby trembled and clung closer, her fingers kneading into the hard muscles of his back. Josh moved again. . .and again. . .and again. And, in a fevered fusing of flesh, an urgent rush of desire, thrust her headlong, spiralling and spinning, into glorious oblivion.

'Are you intending to run the *Calinargo* in place of the *Hummingbird*?' Abby enquired, a long time later.

Josh kissed her brow. 'No. According to my

sources, there's been a steady surge in tourists over the past six months so I figure there's room enough for two. If that meets with your approval?'

'It does.'

He gave a lazy smile. 'Thank goodness. It's high time we started to agree on cruises.'

'It's also high time I rang my aunt and the airline, and told them I won't be leaving tonight,' Abby said, squinting at her watch.

'Or leaving ever,' he declared. 'At least, not without me beside you as your adored husband.'

She laughed, and dotted her finger on the tip of his nose. 'You sound pretty sure of yourself, mister.'

'I am,' Josh grinned, gazing deep into her eyes. 'It's called sixth sense.'

IT'S NEVER TOO LATE FOR SWEET REVENGE . . .

Adrianne's glittering lifestyle was the perfect foil for he
extraordinary talents. A modern princess, flitting from
one exclusive gathering to another, no one knew her a
The Shadow, the most notorious jewel thief of the
decade. With a secret ambition to carry out the
ultimate heist, Adriane had a spectacular plan – one
that would even an old and bitter score. But she woul
need all her stealth and cunning to pull it off – Philip
Chamberlain, Interpol's toughest cop and once a
renowned thief himself was catching up with her. His
only mistake was to fall under Adrianne's seductive
spell.

Published: October 12th **Price: £3.5**

WORLDWIDE

Available from Boots, Martins, John Menzies, W.H. Smith, Woolworths and other paperback stockists.

Also available from Reader Service, P.O. Box 236, Thornton Road, Croydon, Surrey, CR9 3RU.

Zodiac Wordsearch
Competition

How would you like a years supply of Mills & Boon Romances ABSOLUTELY FREE?

Well, you can win them! All you have to do is complete the word puzzle below and send it into us by Dec 31st 1990. The first five correct entries picked out of the bag after this date will each win a years supply of Mills & Boon Romances (Six books every month - worth over £100!) What could be easier?

S	E	C	S	I	P	R	I	A	M	F
I	U	L	C	A	N	C	E	R	L	I
S	A	I	N	I	M	E	G	N	S	R
C	A	P	R	I	C	O	R	N	U	E
S	E	I	R	A	N	G	I	S	I	O
Z	O	D	W	A	T	E	R	B	R	I
O	G	A	H	M	A	T	O	O	A	P
D	R	R	T	O	U	N	I	R	U	R
I	I	B	R	O	R	O	M	G	Q	O
A	V	I	A	N	U	A	N	C	A	C
C	E	L	E	O	S	T	A	R	S	S

Pisces	Aries	Leo	Earth
Cancer	Gemini	Virgo	Star
Scorpio	Taurus	Fire	Sign
Aquarius	Libra	Water	Moon
Capricorn	Sagittarius	Zodiac	Air

Please turn over for entry details

How to enter

All the words listed overleaf, below the word puzzle, are hidden in the grid. You can can find them by reading the letters forwards, backwards, up and down, or diagonally. When you find a word, circle it, or put a line through it. After you have found all the words, the left-over letters will spell a secret message that you can read from left to right, from the top of the puzzle through to the bottom.

Don't forget to fill in your name and address in the space provided and pop this page in an envelope (you don't need a stamp) and post it today. Competition closes Dec 31st 1990.

Only one entry per household (more than one will render the entry invalid).

Mills & Boon Competition
Freepost
P.O. Box 236
Croydon
Surrey CR9 9EL

Hidden message ______________________________

____

Are you a Reader Service subscriber. **Yes** ❑ **No** ❑

Name ______________________________

Address ______________________________

____

____

______________________________ **Postcode** ______________________________

You may be mailed with other offers as a result of entering this competition.
If you would prefer not to be mailed please tick the box. No ❑

COMP9